Medieval in LA

Medieval in

LA

A Fiction

JIM PAUL

COUNTERPOINT

WASHINGTON, D.C.

This book is a work of fiction. Names, characters, places, and
incidents either are products of the author's imagination or
are used fictitiously. Any resemblance to actual events or
locales or persons, living or dead, is entirely coincidental.

Library of Congress Cataloging-in-Publication Data
Paul, Jim, 1950–
    Medieval in LA: a fiction / Jim Paul.
      1. City and town life—California—Los Angeles—Fiction.
    2. Americans—Travel—California—Los Angeles—Fiction.
    3. Medievalists—California—Los Angeles—Fiction. 4. Philosophy,
Medieval—Fiction. I. Title.
PS3566.A82624M43   1996
813'.54—dc20   95-48325
ISBN 1-887178-15-5 (acid-free paper)

FIRST PRINTING

Book design by David Bullen
Composition by Wilsted & Taylor

Printed in the United States of America on acid-free paper that
meets the American National Standards Institute Z39-48
Standard.

COUNTERPOINT
P.O. Box 65793
Washington, D.C. 20035-5793

Distributed by Publishers Group West

CONTENTS

Day

Night

Day

Medieval in

LA

Day

The Tomato Juice Suckhole

I happened to spill tomato juice on myself on the plane. We were somewhere over San Simeon, about halfway to LA and about six miles up. As usual the uproar of the hurtling machine was having nearly no effect inside the cabin. Out there might be frigid, howling death, but in here it was as calm as an eighteenth-century sunroom. The rising sun cast a dozen beams through the plane's left-hand windows, and the tone of the engines lulled me, even. I took my one sip of the juice and opened my book, a volume about the rise of the modern mind in the West. As always, chaos was proceeding.

While I had been reading—oddly enough—that couplet about Newton by Alexander Pope, water molecules were condensing on the cold plastic of my cup. My grip was probably already slipping when maybe the plane hit a bump in the air, something you need to think about only when you are going five hundred miles per hour—even those Miss Budweiser boats don't go five hundred miles an hour—and my thumb lost the edge of the cup.

Then a dumb thing demanded my whole attention: tomato juice in midair over my lap. The nearly full cup struck my open book and dumped out its contents. Most of the fluid funneled into the spine, then poured onto the tray, and dropped at several points into my lap, which was clad—as if for definitive contrast—in white cotton pants. I made a quacking noise and gestured for help.

$\mathfrak{I}$n the next seat, my friend Les could not take notice of the spill, engaged as she was in controlling the airplane. That we sat in coach among the other passengers, that an experienced pilot was in the cockpit, that the airplane itself was the product of decades of modern, trial-and-error engineering was of no consequence whatever to her. She couldn't worry about spilled tomato juice at a time like that, or in any way allow my writhing to distract her from the effort of keeping this enormous machine aloft.

I reached up, the cold juice already chilling my thighs, and pressed the little orange icon for the attendant. The icon was the abstracted form of a human being holding a cup, the head just a dot above the shoulders. Very soon the attendant herself appeared, kneeling by my seat and pointing a shiny nylon knee at me. She wore a strange outfit in a huge herringbone pattern of black and white and yellow.

"Towels," I said. "Juice," and in a minute a fistful of paper towels appeared, a few of which I stuffed into my book. The rest I used to blot up the puddles in the folds of my pants. I'd never liked those pants. I was wearing them only because they seemed right for LA, and now they were so much worse. The juice had already separated into thin yellow fluid, which had penetrated the fabric, and lots of tiny tomato fibers, which had banked up on the surface like flotsam after a flood. I daubed at the mess, then got up, opened the overhead compartment, and pulled a pair of purple nylon volleyball shorts out of my bag. They were what else I had.

"Suckhole," I was thinking by then. "Suckhole" is my friend Harry's word for a stupid accident that ends up altering the future you had in mind. Usually suckholes are minor: You have to count your change before you can get on the bus, and the future changes while you are standing there counting. You go into a bank to get change, meet someone in line, and decide to have lunch. Or the bank is being robbed, and at the very least you have to be interviewed afterward by the police, and stand around for hours as some sergeant takes everybody's statements. Or you get taken hostage and held for so long that you decide to ingratiate yourself with the bank robbers by becoming one, and end up doing time, and so years pass before you find yourself back at the bus stop, dubious enough by then of the efficacy of your own beloved intentions to be carrying the proper change, at least.

The immediate ramification of the tomato juice suckhole in which I found myself on the airplane was a series of fashion decisions. I, who a minute before had been considering Alexander Pope, now had to wonder whether just changing into the shorts would be enough for LA. Dark socks with volleyball shorts was probably dorky. And I probably shouldn't wear a button-down shirt with a sporty lower half, at least not on Melrose Avenue.

No, I decided, I had to change everything. I took a whole wad of clothing plus shoes and went forward to the bathrooms in first class. They were both OCCUPIED, and so I stood there soaked, gazed upon mildly by representatives of the plane's upper class, and trying not to show any attitude. That's right, my crotch has been doused with tomato juice. I'm not happy about it, but I'm not sorry, either.

The stupid thing—among the stupid things, anyway— was that I had been drinking the tomato juice strictly out of habit. When I don't want to drink anything on a plane, I always drink tomato juice. Once it might have cured that deaf-in-a-new-town syndrome, its acidity keeping my ears clear on the landing. I didn't know. I only knew I would never drink it on a plane again. The stuff was too dense for those tippy plastic tumblers.

At last one tiny bathroom was VACANT, and I went in and stripped—the suckhole-in-progress sense much more powerful now that I stood naked, six miles in the air. Nothing seemed impossible at that point. I could only hope that the flight would conclude in LA at least, now that I was dressing for it. Right place, wrong time, it would turn out.

Then back in my seat I still had to deal with my book, which appeared to have been gored and bandaged. I'd spilled the juice on pages 298 and 299, the middle of a chapter called "The Triumph of Secularism," which had begun by describing the outcome of the medieval church's misbegotten sponsorship of Scholasticism—an enormous historical suckhole, I could see now—when Thomas Aquinas, thinking that the exercise of reason would buttress the foundations of faith, inadvertently opened the door to those bewigged men of the eighteenth century in whose reasonable universe God would be, as one of them said later, "an unnecessary hypothesis."

The juice had soaked through several pages summarizing events from the burning of Giordano Bruno through the so-called Enlightenment, including a quote from miserable Pascal, uttered in the grip of his own spiritual crisis as he found himself passing through a vortex between being devout and being mathematical. Sucked into the new void, he'd said, "I am terrified by the eternal silence of these infinite spaces."

The first time I'd read this, I recalled, I'd been mildly annoyed by what seemed its overstatement, its absolute adjectives. Why all this fuss about living in the actual world? I'd thought. Now though, covered with tomato juice, Pascal seemed less authoritative and altogether more sympathetic.

Once a cat I lived with in my student days had thrown up on an open page of the *Norton Anthology*. I had taken a break from an awful reading assignment to feed the animal—any excuse would have done, really—and had given her a new kind of cat food with crab in it. The cat ate, followed me back into the study, hopped up on the desk, and barfed almost immediately on the tale of Melibeus and his good wife Prudence. Chaucer's only prose treatise, this work is so long and dull that even really stodgy scholars consider it unsuccessful. "A litel thyng in prose," begins the teller of this tale, who then proceeds for eight thousand words. The incident with the cat had proven all for the best, though. Grossly defaced, the text suddenly flourished with irony. The work was just stuffing, I had to believe after that, insulation from the censors and Chaucer's sly revenge upon them.

I recalled that incident, looking at this tomato juice disaster. At its epicenter, where the bomb had struck, was the couplet I had paused over at the moment of the explosion. "Nature and nature's laws lay hid in night," it read there beneath the tomato microswamp. "God said let Newton be, and all was light."

Pre-Copernican

In the next seat my friend Les was still concentrating on keeping the plane aloft. "How's it going?" I asked her. She was worried about turbulence on landing, she said. I took her hand, which was clammy.

"Don't worry," I said, knowing she wouldn't listen. "They've done this a billion times."

So had I, I thought. I'd spent so much time psyching out the moment, sipping juice I didn't want without tasting it, because it might magically help. There I was, sitting in an aisle seat, altogether elsewhere, ready to get on to my next bit of plan. But the lapful of cold juice and the irony of the swollen text had awakened me, at least momentarily, and I remembered what travel used to feel like, that half-frightening certainty that everything would be different in a new place, especially myself. When I'd first flown, I'd spent every flight pressed to the window, amazed at the earth and sky.

Beyond my companion was an empty window seat. "Do you mind if I move?" I said. I abandoned the soaked book and slid over.

That day the Pacific had no relief and looked like a vast blue plate trimmed with the thinnest edge of white. When the plane's straight flight path found land again, we flew over the long-shadowed ridges of the coastal range, and the sea hung in midwindow like a porcelain band. Day was proceeding out there, I thought, going thataway, west across the water. Then I recalled this wasn't true.

Oh, Copernicus, what did you know? The sun still rose and set, still went west, over the ocean, five hundred years after you proved it didn't. If the parade of the heavens were just the backward projection of our own movement, if humanity had been displaced from its old seat, front and center, mostly the news hadn't gotten around. Lots of people still believed in astrology, for instance, never mind that it described a universe that no longer existed, that the constellations of the zodiac didn't circle the earth, didn't rise and fall, didn't wax and wane.

Below me the ocean opened as we crossed the coast then closed again as we plunged back inland over the stark peaks around the Grapevine, and I began to approach something like the thought that had been occurring to me when I'd spilled the juice. We have all this information about the actual world, centuries of it since the scientific idea had taken hold, yet we still live mostly in the old realm, at the center of our own universe, finding our significance, manifesting our intentions.

Maybe I could still join the modern world, I thought. I'd only be five hundred years late. Look out this window, I challenged myself, and imagine being actual—or at least not pre-Copernican. Consider, for instance, that this coast is falling away beneath a still sun, that the navigator of the jet is probably making some adjustments to account for LA's eastward movement during the hour that we'd been in the air. Take seriously, for that matter, that being alive on the earth all my life had been not so different from being on the plane—living in the steady, adequately lighted reality we had constructed to enable our plans, a purely human place, not the actual world.

It was no use, though. These ideas, to be honest, seemed like feathers in a hat band, mere decor. I wasn't about to plunge, Pascal-like, through some vortex. I knew where I lived, no matter what I thought. Though I didn't explicitly believe in God or astrology—for instance—I knew that I dwelt nonetheless amid the old assurance, as surely as if I could still hear the music of the spheres. Secularism hadn't yet triumphed, at least in my head. Apollo might as well still drive his flaming chariot, and if tomato juice spilled on my lap, it would mean something. I might as well be medieval, I was thinking. A man from the Middle Ages, flying over the ocean and across the sky.

The plane surpassed a last ridge and descended, belly first, into the broad LA basin, which was filled to a distinct level with a goldish broth of urban air. The jets changed tone, and my companion, who hates the sound of the engines slowing down on a plane, gripped my forearm with her cold, damp hand as we turned westward on our approach toward LAX. Straight down there, as we banked, was downtown LA, like somebody's collection of architectural models. As we popped up again, I got a last glimpse of the beach, the ocean no longer unrelieved, the individual waves visible, darker lines out to sea breaking into white as they made land. It could seem to be an amazing coincidence that the waves always found the land at sea level, I thought idly, though they had to. That was what sea level was.

I left it at that for the moment, turning my attention to my pretty, chestnut-haired friend. Les was happy to be back on the ground, and revived, as if her faith alone had delivered us through the ordeal of flight.

Trace Element

At last count, the proportions of matter to emptiness in the universe stood at a tenth of a poppy seed to a sphere the size of the earth. All stuff amounted to an infinitesimal smidgen in the scale of things, and of that bit, the heavier matter such as carbon composed just a trace element. The glass and linoleum of airport corridors, the Sierra Nevada, the air I'd just flown through, the stone that Samuel Johnson kicked—the entire planet itself was the tiniest trace of this trace, and of that minuteness, living matter stood on the scale similarly diminished, humanity an exponential step smaller still. My own life was some billionth part of this larger life, and the moment I was experiencing just then some billionth of that, and not even an important bit. Taking these cosmic densities seriously,

I'd have to admit that by any human measure of significance, the moment didn't matter. I didn't, either. Nothing much did.

Just then I stood above my friend and among the other travelers descending an escalator. The various airport scenes opened and closed below us with the smoothness of a tracking camera. All of us seemed present enough and life sized. By now even escalators and air travel seemed routine, barely noticeable, and long, long ago we'd dismissed the suspicion that life as we know it can't be.

I was feeling regular enough at this point. I hadn't the slightest doubt of my own actual existence, never mind the odds. Despite the tomato juice suckhole, my intentions still seemed inviolate. We had plans, simple plans for the weekend, and these enlarged me most of all, transforming whatever resounding cosmic depths into so much painted backdrop. We would rent a car, drive to Hollywood, stay with Jess and her husband, Steve, attend a birthday party that evening, and spend the next day at the beach.

We had a procedure. We had talked, we had decided, we had looked into each other's eyes, and come up with this plan. This was what mattered just then, and life was a matter of mattering, not just of matter.

Such thoughts and the thin purple shorts I was wearing gave me a nice feeling of lightness as I passed through the crowd around the baggage carousels, a mote in a sunbeam, a fleck of gold leaf adrift in the millenia, out through the whooshing automatic doors and beyond, into the bright, briny air. Besides, trace element of a trace element of a trace element that I was anyway, what did it matter which era I took for home? I could just float along, my baggage just carry-on, medieval perhaps, but also almost nonexistent and happily so.

The Time Tourist

Hence I could be the casual time tourist on the rent-a-car bus, watching the landscape of twentieth-century transportation go by—the airport loop, the parking garages, the buses and taxis. It didn't, oddly enough, seem incompatible with my medieval mind. The airport with its indications and portals and conveyances felt familiar, habitual even. There might be an enormous cosmos out there, an ample arena where something larger than human meaning was happening, but this wasn't it. This was dense, technological California, every square foot intense with low-level significance, an engineered environment.

Maybe it wasn't possible to put aside meaning, even if life might be roomier without it. A friend of mine jokes about parking karma. Live a certain way, think the right thoughts, and you can get a space to materialize right in front of your destination, he says, as if virtue could give you an edge on city traffic. When my friend speaks of this, he talks half-seriously, though I can tell some part of him—his medieval part—believes. Irony is good for talking about parking karma, allowing you to cling to the magic and still be modern.

For me, even trivial coincidences gather weight. In a restaurant, I might speak a word in conversation and hear it spoken simultaneously—or almost—at another table. Maybe the speaker over there heard my word subconsciously, and as it happened more or less to fit, took it for his own conversation. Maybe, with my ears tuned up for the word, I just happened to hear its accidental repetition. Or maybe, weirdly, the word somehow was floating by, wending along in the ether of the collective unconscious and lodging at that moment in both our minds.

Whatever, I can't dismiss it, and neither—at least in some more suggestible state—can I entirely put aside the sense that the reiteration itself is significant somehow, illuminating this trivial word as a sign, as further evidence for the mysterious order of things, for fate, whether it's parking karma or God. Never mind. I hearken. I listen up. I need that parking space. I need it enough to wonder when one magically opens up for me, right in front, just what I did right that day.

We have minds that make connections, willy-nilly, and worse, that have to. The firmness of how things turn out, the silent testimony for what doesn't, not to mention our own need to exist for a reason, all these press the case for fate, for an order conceived in retrospect and raised toward the future, like a headlight. This we might call medieval thinking, making the next thing always the right thing, even if horribly so. There's always a thread; in fact there's thread all over the place.

$\mathcal{A}$round me on the bus, my friend and these travelers, Disneyland-bound families mostly, rode patiently, awaiting their reasonable, minor fates at the end of the ride with the passivity of bus passengers everywhere. David Hume, a sanguinary enough Scottish gentleman of the eighteenth century, had argued that we could not know what—if any-thing—lay beyond our sensory impressions. There was no way, Hume proposed, to know what was really there, or how events were bound. All contingency, all commonality might simply arise only from an individual's habit of per-ceiving things that way. This was great stuff, I thought, maybe even epistemologically sound, though impossible to feel on that sunny, placid bus.

Maybe, out of the womb, we took up previous minds and accreted our way to the present moment in layers of histori-cal thought, ways of perceiving that never really improved or replaced one another, but continued to coexist as parallel explanations. If so, maybe some people had proceeded to the present age with its limited certainties and Humey possibil-ities. My own accretion, though, seemed to have reached only the Middle Ages. I could feel that I had a mind ages older, still calm as if in the knowledge that Hume had it wrong.

This thought made me feel that way, anyway, as calm in my own nearly completed millennium as some big-eyed monk beneath a halo. The Middle Ages might still live on, in some ways more popular than ever, just as the Beats still do readings in North Beach. And I'd been there—lived there, it turned out. This little Copernican game I'd played with myself on the plane—that I might live in the roomy new world, that I might be actual, existing actually on the moving earth, for one thing—this was just one more fanciful conception. I had one philosophy, undisplaced because I had never actually considered it as such. Mine was the snug medieval model.

I'd been poring over my own little universe like a monk over a manuscript, it seemed then. Regular events I'd divined no less steadily and faithfully as those attendant on the miracles and omens, the signs and wonders of yore. For me, things stood as around some Gothic altar, the saints appearing each in a panel, juxtaposed in symmetries, their cloaks and large-eyed faces, their customary props—a book, a skull—in primary colors and gold. Though the figures themselves might stand in midstory, the moments previous and following—also the relations among these singular tales—needed no depiction, as clear to the faithful as the trodden pilgrims' way.

Theatricum Botanicum

Louise and Lloyd walk a lot, in a neighborhood where no one walks. Walking the dog, ostensibly, they leave their home—a typical apartment building for LA, two stories around a garden court, like a cloister, where the Staffordshire terrier Shantah buries her bones in the flower pots on the patio—and stroll up the palmy, gridded slope of Los Feliz toward Griffith Park. Just then they gleamed powerfully in my memory, vivid in the lost opportunity to see them that weekend: mustached and ironic Lloyd, vivacious, Lauren Bacallesque Louise, these two and their brindled, adoring pit bull on the sidewalk beneath the palms.

At home, caught in the riptide of city life, I felt lucky to be able to see a friend once in six months, to fix those moments in our schedules. But Louise's letters and the skip of telephone calls between the three of us had sustained our relations for years. It seemed by then that Louise and Lloyd, four hundred miles away, knew me more intimately than did my nearest neighbors. Shocking to think it, I had probably even actually spent more time with those two, on the two or three trips I made yearly to LA, than I did with many of my friends at home.

I'd met Louise ten years before, in a job interview. She was the interviewee, and I was on a volunteer board at a small art gallery that was seeking a director. A few of us had taken over the organization in the middle of a crisis, most of the previous board having fled in panic over the finances. It was the first time I'd been on the other side of an interview, and I was nervous. Louise was impressive. She had written a book on performance art. She knew Ping Chong and Meredith Monk. She'd lived in Seattle and Portland and LA, and had done similar work in those cities. By the end of the interview, she was already telling me what we should do next, and I was praying that she would take the job.

We dated, even, a couple of times after that, though nothing came of it. She had a boyfriend in LA. We went out and had a good time, and the moment passed, for some reason—psychology, fate, mere coincidence—when we might have taken off in the serious-relationship direction. After that, we could talk about anything, though, and we became great friends.

Lloyd was the boyfriend in LA. When he had first visited San Francisco to see her, we had eyed each other. But Lloyd was so smart and goofy that I soon had to think of him as a relative. Eventually Louise moved to LA to marry him.

I'd gone down for their wedding, which was held the day after that night game when Kirk Gibson hit his impossible home run and limped around the bases—pumping his arm between second and third—to beat the Oakland A's in the World Series against the Dodgers. I'd watched the game in a hotel room in LA, the sound of cheering Dodger fans audible through the walls on both sides. The image of Lasorda leaping out of the dugout, that roar, on TV and right next door, which sounded like all of joyous Los Angeles shouting, and the dejected A's—my team—this stuck with me through that weekend.

The next day was a day of bad wildfires in the San Gabriel Mountains. Louise and Lloyd had their wedding at Will Geer's Shakespeare stage—called the Theatricum Botanicum—a wooded amphitheater above the city in Topanga Canyon. A bust of Geer, appearing as he did as the grandfather on *The Waltons*, overlooked the pavilion. I'd driven up there and had stood amidst the trees as Louise and Lloyd had materialized on a little hillock above the assembled guests and then, as from Olympus, had descended the forested slope to the stage, there to take their vows.

Tiny, white particles of ash streamed out of the atmosphere, falling in perfect vertical lines like fine confetti on the bride and groom, on the guests and the rabbi, on the bronze head of Will Geer, and on me. The rabbi sang a lot, exuberantly, joyously. I had a terrible headache and knew that I hadn't ever—until that moment—quite relinquished my feelings for Louise, though now that events had so composed themselves, I had to. My head hurt, though.

Once I'd told Louise that my family still called me

"Jimmy." She'd liked this diminutive and started calling me by it. After a while Lloyd did, too. I got to like Lloyd, to like him a lot. It was impossible that the man wouldn't grow on you, actually. Louise was no fool. The last time I went to LA, he and I had just hung around at his studio, and he'd told me stories all afternoon.

But I wouldn't be visiting that Los Angeles on this trip. Louise and Lloyd's LA would exist just in my memory this time. There were millions of LAs, an infinite fan of super-imposed cities, each one thrown out from somebody's perception and memory. Every bit of town, every sunny facade and piece of street litter and palm frond, had to be illuminated by personal significance, to seem to collude in some-one's fate somehow, or else never get noticed at all, never in some sense exist. This thought gave me my first, uneasy, ongoing-tomato-juice-suckhole sensation of the weekend.

I gazed out the bus window, looking for something that might resolve this vague disquiet, and settled for the white structure just then streaming by, the jet-age icon of LAX, which I'd always taken to be the control tower. That build-ing's elevated, podlike body rolled past the upper windows of the bus. It had an ovoid main element and was imbedded on a thick column beneath parabolic arches. Just then, it looked like an insect or a fancy hi-fi.

Back in the gleaming fifties, the structure had been fu-turistic. Now it was famous from TV, from detective shows, one image in a sequence including the wheels emerging from the belly of the plane that indicated arrival in LA. At least, I thought, this landmark appeared in everyone's version of LA, like a spindle through a stack of 45s. Then, as it receded, I noticed that this building wasn't the control tower at all. That tower stood nearby and taller, looking functional and hieroglyphic, bristling with antennae—the fifties' actual future.

The white, futuristic TV icon turned out to have people eating breakfast in it, to be a theme restaurant, and as that old vision of the future swung around the bend, I wondered if authenticity mattered, as far as reality was concerned.

The Seek Function

My own car, a Honda, is ancient, a battered blue citymobile, the tape player shot, the seats flattened, its body dinged and crinkled, the whole thing idiosyncratic, withered by various suckholes, the chief one a weird overamping problem, an electrical-system bug that burns up a battery a year, the last time killing the engine in the middle of an intersection downtown. The sheer force of my will, Harry had said, keeps that car alive.

So the last time I'd gone to LA, I'd rented a new LeBaron and had driven over to Los Feliz in a controlled automotive environment, the soundtrack, the strange and famous town, the car, all contributing to a cinematic effect. I was looking forward to doing that again, to working the buttons, to making the bright town go by, the air-conditioning conditioning the air and the stereo cranked. You could enshrine yourself and your intentions in a car in LA until the experience felt almost like one of those stationary rides at Universal Studios, an interactive machine manipulating projections of the world. I never got this feeling anymore in my car.

The bus driver called out "Emerald Aisle," and we got out and went into a tinted glass hut beneath green banners. At the rental counter, I more or less got what I wanted, though I'd had to talk the clerk out of renting me a Buick.

"What else do you have?" I'd asked.

"A Grand Am," he said. "It's essentially the same car."

Not to me. I liked the epic suggestion in Grand Am. Plus a Pontiac was cool. In 1967, my friend Terry had let me drive his new GTO to summer school sometimes. He had, from his dad, a red convertible with black interior, with a Hearst shifter and an engine the size of Wisconsin. It could snap your head back.

But the generic Pontiac we rented turned out not to be that car. I'd been told it was red, but this red was purplish, a focus-group red. The Pontiac's designers had made just one concession to the old romantic connotations of the car's muscular style. They'd left the inner door panels raw, just stringing them with nets for storage—as if Richard Petty had advised them to rip out all that froufrou and toss it out the window in order to lighten the vehicle for speed.

Still, it had a radio. As I drove out of the lot and headed north across the grid of streets, looking for La Cienega, Les

pushed the seek button, and the radio went through its routine, sampling station after station. I'd rented cars in deso-
late western places, where the seek function just flung itself
out across the emptiness of the dial, and in its orbit found
the same cowboy-want-ads-on-the-air show over and over,
the only signal for a hundred miles. But here in LA, there
were more stations than silence. Hundreds of songs, a multitude of voices arose from the dial. The seek mechanism
took over, giving each station its due, providing just enough
of each song for us to decide whether it reflected our mood.
I heard Sting and Steely Dan and the Pixies and the Four
Seasons—and this just a bit of the white rock and roll
among the crop of other music: pop, funk, classical, soul,
oldies, country, hip-hop, Christian, grunge, easy listening
—tunes in all attitudes and periods, it seemed. It seemed
possible that it was *all* there on the dial, down to the most
microscopic market niche, that I could find Brazilian juju
blues or medieval church music, a soundtrack for my medieval day on the station playing All Gregorian Chant, All
the Time.

Soon we were riding along, just as I'd wished, with just
the proper soundtrack. The radio search even turned up a
coincidence, a synchronicity in the form of a jazz sax, Sonny
Stitt's, playing "Scrapple from the Apple." I'd been reading
about Stitt just the day before, on my job at the Museum
of Modern Art in San Francisco. Doing research, I'd come
across a description of postwar LA, a time when jazz legends
and European exiles and proto-Beats and stars of the golden
age of Hollywood had come together to make those few
years seem to be one of the best times ever—Ingrid Berg-

man and Charlie Parker and Wallace Berman and Bertolt Brecht in town, the war won, the air clear as glass to the hills. LA had flowers as big as trees, Brecht had said somewhere.

And here I was, and here was Stitt on the radio, and I couldn't help feeling favored by fortune in a way that made no sense. There was an order, however odd, to which I belonged. It was sheer randomness, I knew, though it made the moment seem like my own, and this, precisely, was the medieval feeling: knowing otherwise, but nevertheless living at the center of the universe, where the music was my music, where everything happened for a reason, where waves of will washed over all.

Just for a moment, as Stitt played, I'd indulge, I thought. I'd steer the world with my whims or at least align myself with forces that did. So for that moment, the morning sun climbed the sky, shining down on me and the other cars with the sympathetic vibration of this jazz sax.

"I was just reading about that guy yesterday," I said, when the song ended.

"Who?" Les asked, and when I told her, made that assenting sound—the staccato "hm"—an acknowledgment, nice enough. I could tell she couldn't feel the coincidence as I did. This was natural—maybe no one could. Maybe such conjoined events could only offer their fated flavor to the person who connected them. I was accidentally tuned to the details, I thought, and I tried to leave it at that.

Seven Times Seven

S o I just drove, letting Les direct me. She wanted to buy flowers for our hosts, as was her habit, and so took us first to Pavilions on Santa Monica Boulevard in West Hollywood, a supermarket with an enormous flower shop in the front. She knew the way, sort of, and we proceeded on a stepwise diagonal of cross streets and avenues, climbing upslope toward the hills, looking for the place.

When we got out of the air-conditioned car, it was already hot at ten in the morning in the big parking lot, though inside the supermarket, it was cool, and even cold among the flowers, when we pushed open the sliding door of the big glass-fronted refrigerator case, that chill air loaded with mixed perfume.

We were looking for lilies. In the case were sylvia lilies

and big white nova lilies and flamingo lilies and yellow lilies called auratum. There were dahlias that looked like scrub brushes, maybe ten shades of gladioli, speckled, open-mouthed orchids, and purple water lilies floating in tubs. Behind us the bank of registers beeped as we picked out a couple of stems of stargazers and a bunch of gorgeous, un-marked pink lilies. Their big tonguelike petals were mottled and pointed and slightly curled, puckered at the edges, and their pale pods glowed with the flower inside. With them we chose tuberoses, which were powerfully fragrant even among the other flowers in the case. The name *tuberose* suggested a cross between a flower and a yam, as if it could be nourishing as well as beautiful.

In the context of my thoughts that weekend, the flowers seemed strange, more exotic than usual. We make what we can of flowers, when we give them or get them, though flowers always end up being more than that, larger than our intentions, beyond us somewhere. Just then, the array of thick blossoms inside the refrigerator case looked extra-terrestrial.

We paid a lot for the flowers and took them back to the car. In the parking lot notices for acting workshops papered the lampposts. The car's interior exhaled heated air when I opened the door. As I pulled out, following Les's directions to Jess and Steve's and looking for the right side street off Santa Monica, the flowers, laid across the back seat, filled the hot car with their sweet incense.

Among the English peasants of the Middle Ages, I re-called, seven was a proverbially big number. A really enormous amount of something was "seven times seven" of it. That was the world you could touch, the world of the child-hood of the West. As for actual children, though, there was little distinction for them then. Perhaps they were all chil-dren. A person of forty was rare and ancient, and that arche-typal relation to God as Augustine saw it—a young and naive child to an infinitely greater, omniscient, and omnip-otent father—not such a feat of abstraction. To such a mind, what could be farther than the actual London, which might be just over the hill? What could be nearer than the Jerusa-lem of the stories?

We found their street, Sweetzer, and turned down it. That was the Middle Ages, I was thinking, but were we any larger now? In a way, we were, our telescopes having vastly expanded the universe. This, though, only made us feel smaller, of course. Logarithmically—I remembered—the average human being stood midway in size between the atoms and the galaxies. A little more than halfway, actually. Maybe it had simply turned out that God spoke in expo-nents. Never mind that we had to proceed one by one by one, I thought as I looked for the address.

Where I had actually lived wasn't so vast. Seven times seven could still seem like a big number. I had lived my life from event to event, linking them in my personal sense of recognition and coincidence. And this tale of the universe with its ninety-three million miles to the sun, for instance, remained one story among others, some of which were older and more cogent as art. What was the enormous, thermonuclear center of the solar system, anyway, com-pared to this humane feature of the day, the sun I could feel at that moment, warm through the windshield, old Sol who rose in the morning? There was one sun, not one

among billions, and one me. I said "sunrise," anyway
—though it didn't—and when the next thing happened,
I could without much effort claim it as personal, as my
fate.

I found the right number and pulled up.

Sound in a Bell Is but Trembling Motion

In 1323—the year the Church canonized the fat monk Thomas Aquinas—the pope summoned to his palace a gaunt English friar, one Brother William of Ockham. Brother William made the journey on foot across France to Avignon, there to stand trial. His former chancellor at Oxford, John Lutterell, had submitted fifty-six excerpts from Ockham's writings to the papal court, indicting them for heresy.

A place of white towers and oranges and brocade, Avignon was then also the center of the Western world. The papacy had been imported from Italy to Provence just fourteen years before, when Pope Clement V, a Frenchman, had refused to go to Rome to claim his seat. Clement feared reprisal from the Romans who had sworn revenge for the death of his predecessor, Pope Boniface, that aged pontiff assaulted and kidnapped by French agents in 1303.

This new French pope felt safer, naturally enough, in Avignon, which was not in France, *per se*, but nonetheless under French sway. Back in Rome it was whispered that he also had a mistress, Catherine of Perigord, in Provence. In any case, his choice of Avignon initiated an era of great luxury and worldly power for the Church in this floral southern town, which would remain the center of the universe, more or less, for six successive papal terms.

At the time the Church was engaged in the world, selling, for instance, pieces of the True Cross. Enough of these wooden bits and splinters were circulating in Europe, just then, to build an ark. Besides such merchandise, the Church was also offering up for sale any and all favors and benefits it might confer. Clerical offices and preferments, forgiveness of sins, pardons for crimes—all went to the highest bidder.

The money received for these goods and services poured into Avignon by the cartload. And where money went, fashion followed. That year, decked out with his friends in purple robes and perfumes, the nineteen-year-old Petrarch sallied forth, seeking a ladylove and dodging the pigs in the streets, mingling there with the merchants and ambassadors, the churchmen and aspirants from across the continent, buyers and middlemen attracted by the Church's lucrative trade.

The money itself, in gold and silver, piled up on the floors of the Papal Palace, where gaggles of brokers and clerics thumbed it, counting out loud. Beneath the pope's new bedchamber, which had hunting scenes painted on the walls, a trapdoor opened to a narrow stairway, where the pope might descend, on a midnight whim, to sit in his treasury among the shining stacks of his gold.

The day William of Ockham arrived in this hustling, stylish town, he walked through its crenellated white gates wearing the gray habit of Saint Francis, a garment in which, it was widely believed then, you could not enter Hell. Dying nobles had themselves wrapped in Franciscan robes: The Devil himself wouldn't take you, thus clad. Originally renowned for its purity of spirit, the Franciscan order embodied its founder's vow of poverty. Franciscans were to possess nothing, to wander the earth doing good and begging for the means to live, though for food and necessities only, never for cash.

This reputation for purity eventually corrupted the order, a paradox in which Ockham might have glimpsed his own paradoxical fate. When one flung riches from the deathbed, at the last, what purer place to throw them than to these threadbare brethren of Saint Francis? Such guilty largesse, by the fourteenth century, had enriched the Franciscan friars, many of whom, fallen from their founder's austere ideal, were wearing fur and jewels and eating meat, some even keeping jesters and hunting with falcons. Chaucer's friar takes a good pittance for his penance; Boccaccio's sells a wing feather from the Archangel Gabriel.

But Brother William was a true Franciscan. Having renounced all earthly pleasures, endorsing a life of complete poverty, he acted always in the original spirit of the order. He had also taken up lifelong intellectual combat with the new forces in the Church. For one thing, he denied papal infallibility: Nothing on earth was certain; no one on earth was infallible. Formidable in a fight, he took up his battle on the grounds of philosophy. Humble monk though he might appear, he was a writer of note, a reasoner of wide repute, and had made himself a specialist in logic, which happened to be his opponent's new weapon of choice. "The Concordian," as the now Saint Thomas Aquinas had been called, was Ockham's real opponent. Ockham himself was known as "The Invincible Doctor."

The pope's agents detained Ockham under house arrest in the palace for five years altogether, as his case moved glacially through its legal process. The trial itself didn't start right away. After the initial debates, the questionings and blandishments, a full trial might not have proven necessary after all. The pope had ordered his intellectual combatants to take up Ockham's philosophical objections, which engaged those very principles of Thomist thought now enshrined in the Church with the apotheosis of Aquinas himself.

Fifty years earlier, as a member of the Faculty of Arts at the University of Paris, Aquinas had gathered the few early strands of reasoning technique into a new method of comparing opinions, using the linguistic, semantic, and logical tools rediscovered in Aristotle two hundred years earlier. At the time that Aquinas first ordered them translated and studied, the natural philosophy and metaphysics of Aristotle were still officially banned by the Church. By the time of Aquinas's death in 1274, all the Aristotelian tools had been doctrinally sanctioned. Schooled in their use, some clerics had begun to categorize reality in a way that would come to be known as scientific. In assuming this Greek method for Christianity, Aquinas, "the Concordian," had contended that the rational analysis of nature would affirm revelation and provide a further basis for faith.

This impulse Ockham sought to block. He aimed to re-store the Church, to halt its drift toward materialism by arguing, logically, grammatically—that is, in the new Aris-totelian terms—that no inference could be drawn from the earthly world of unique individuals about the nature of God, who was universal, infinite, and knowable only via revelation. Natural experience imposed strict limits on knowledge.

God caused everything in the first place, was always everything's first and sufficient cause, Ockham argued. Earthly causation was always secondary, and God could suspend its operation at any time. For all we knew, for all we could know, it was God's instantaneous will that connected spark to flame. Nor was God at any time restricted simply to such earthly causation. He could enable a body to be in two places at one time, for instance, or give knowledge of the nonexistent. The actual order would always be contin-gent, Ockham reasoned, whereas the possible order would always be beyond contingency. And God alone knew all possible orders, including the actual one.

In these opinions, Brother William would not be moved. After a year, it became apparent to the clerics that Ockham would submit neither to luxury nor to threat, and the trial went forward. Then in ponderous course they found him guilty, censuring his writings, deeming his views heretical, also false, dangerous, erroneous, rash, and contradictory. They could not of course answer his every point, but they could and did condemn him.

Still, Brother William's demonstration of the power of Aristotelian method was to prove paradoxically victorious. After his trial Ockham's opponents studied his writings carefully and, grasping the rigor of his argument, took it to buttress the assertion that science might proceed without fear of contradicting doctrine, nature admitting no dependable clue to God in any case.

Thus the way parted. Engorged with both science and doctrine, the Church wobbled for an ungainly moment, until 1513 when Copernicus published his heliocentric theories and exploded its very cosmos. By then Ockham's method was known—this the profoundest irony—as the *via moderna*, as opposed to the *via antiqua* of Aquinas.

Ockham's was a quantum leap. He had argued that nothing in the world corresponded to universality; that all worldly things were completely individual. Ockham's razor, therefore, was simply this: One may not multiply things beyond necessity. You had to start with the specific and work toward the universal, though you would arrive there only through revelation, not through exercise of reason.

Human understanding, Ockham insisted, had very narrow limits. God's scale was infinite, ours minute, and with our earthly minds, we could not presume to make the connection. We were, in fact, utterly contingent upon God, our reality hinging every instant upon God's mysterious will.

So Ockham would have turned humanity away from reason and science, and back toward revelation and trembling faith in the omnipotent Creator.

But in this effort he was mistaken. For science, deemed secular and cut off, did quite well, thank you, out in the fields and on its own, peddling its modest sureties and practical applications. And the spirit of philosophy, too, departed with science after that, now equipped with this sparkling new tool, inductive reasoning, Ockham's razor, still sharp for Hume four hundred years after Ockham stropped it.

Miraculously, Brother William managed to escape from Avignon after his trial. Under cover of dark he and his confreres somehow slipped the palace guards, or at least slipped them something, then stole horses and rode for their lives to Pisa. There Ockham swore allegiance to the German emperor and fired back an indictment of his own, charging the pope with seventy errors and seven heresies. Duly excommunicated, Brother William continued his life-long struggle for the soul of the Church, putting his effort into the expedient cause of the secular state. Another tactical error this would prove, over the centuries. There would be no going back.

Ockham died in 1349, the third year of the Black Death. Back in Avignon, the pope managed to survive. His doctors ordered him to sit between bonfires of frankincense and myrrh all through that steaming summer in Provence. The holy perfume had no effect, of course, but the huge heat kept His Holiness from others, even from fleas.

Mobile

To me, the comforting thing about history and philosophy was the seeming firmness they lent to the present moment, though such a glance worked best slightly sidewise, I'd found. There on the pavement in front of Jess and Steve's, having arrived for the moment anyway at some firm, even obdurate sense of human reality—dry above the wash of centuries—I was allowed, even forced, to impute such firmness to the moment, though almost any scrutiny of the actual could manage to turn it into a wisp of wisps.

Just then it was the complex smell of the side street—cut grass, oleander, and gardenia scent in the hot, slightly metallic air, a particular LA infusion—that touched off a memory from the fifties of myself as a child, aged about eight, amazed to be in California at last. My mother had brought

me back to show me to her parents, old southerners, Ala-
bamans who'd migrated to Los Angeles earlier in the century. I could smell that old strangeness—and these people
my own family—in that day's urban bouquet, even detect
deep in it somewhere my childish excitement about Disneyland, which I had been promised for behaving on the
long car trip across the country.

In 1929, my grandfather found work in California as a
beachfront hotel manager, and came west on the train from
Mobile, bringing everyone, a dozen people, not just his wife
and sons and daughters, but her mother and aunts and un-
cles, even a pair of German in-laws, all that remained of an
old Confederate family, from Mobile. In the Civil War, my
grandfather's father had commanded the cadets defending
the University of Alabama. They'd surrendered in the end
to the veteran Union troops, who burned the library. In the
years that followed, the sons dispersed, this one in particular going south to Mobile, then seeking a new start in the
Far West.

He had sent his eldest boy, John, then just eight, down to
the Southern Pacific station to buy the family's tickets. En
route, my mother, who was the littlest one, stepped off the
train during a stop at Albuquerque, and hopped barefoot
across the hot ground, as the family laughed. After World
War II, she'd gone to Berkeley where she'd met my father
on a blind date. And I'd grown up in DC, where my father
took a job with the Kennedy administration.

So on vacations I was taken out west, back home to LA.
We crowded their terra-cotta-roofed bungalow in Pasadena, and I was presented to my ancient grandfather, a hair-
less, severe, and pious man with a southerner's formality,
who seemed to approve of me, conditionally. When they'd

come to California from the South, they'd sought to bring whatever little bit of it with them that they could, and so their yard smelled of gardenias, which I decided was the triggering ingredient in the smell there, in front of Jess and Steve's. This was the long chain of association, a century and more of human striving, evoked in the floral LA scent of that street.

That day, the apartments were being painted, each of the four duplexes a different pastel shade. Dropcloths and scaffolding lined the walkway. At the rear duplex, up two little steps, was their door, which Jess and Steve opened at our knock. A handsome and youthful pair, Jess voluble and dark-eyed, Steve tall and elegant, they met us with a burst of welcome. Inside, their place was shady and clean, under its arched ceilings carefully chosen objects—a Persian rug, a framed Piranesi print of a wild ruin somewhere, a little domestic still life by William Bailey, a glass-topped table with a wrought-iron base in a floral design. We presented them with the flowers. Jess remarked at the big pink lilies, for which we had no name, as they'd had no tag in the store.

Jess and Steve's apartment had a pleasant, meet-you-halfway quality, I thought, with lots of space seemingly left open for new choices or whatever might happen next. We were shown our place in Jess's study, where there was a futon couch. We dropped our bags there and went back out into the kitchen to catch up. At the sink Steve cut the stems of the flowers and put them in a vase as I recounted the events on the plane, using my purple nylon volleyball shorts as a prop and attempting to get control of that suckhole as a story.

$\mathcal{L}$ater I went back into the study again, to unpack. I got the wet book out of my bag and spread it out beneath the window on the floor, where it might dry. On the page I opened, which was somewhere in the damp thick middle, I had underlined a passage. The felt-tip ink had spread a little in the orangy bath. "With Luther," it had read there, "the monolithic structure of the medieval church had cracked. With Copernicus and Galileo, the medieval cosmology it-self had cracked." Not altogether, it said, covered with juice.

Over Jess's desk was a bulletin board, and pinned to it were dozens of mementos: poems and pictures of babies and friends and souvenirs. The room had a computer and a wall of interesting books, including a section for movie scripts— some Jess's own—their abbreviated titles written in Magic Marker across the cut edges, so that the words were sec-tioned horizontally where the pages had spread. The scripts seemed informal, more like memos to directors, sugges-tions for movies.

On the windowsill in the study sat the cat. Black and sleek, she was called Marlene. She had the wacky, lanky look of adolescent cats, but she was as self-possessed as her namesake, and wished just to perch on the sill and watch me. When I tried to stroke her, she cuffed my hand, the touch of one half-withdrawn claw enhancing the feeling I was hav-ing just then of the exact, swift, nearly nonexistent particu-larity of the moment.

$\mathcal{T}$he actual was a mirage, it seemed just then, a shimmer-ing that evaporated as I came near. I remembered a trip I had taken a few years before, to visit Mobile and look for traces of the old family. I'd found the lot on which the house had stood and the huge live oak that had shaded their porch. But the lot was empty; the house was gone. I found a piece of broken brick in the long grass and brought it home. Besides the stories we told ourselves, there were the barest bits to evidence our beginnings.

Real events dissolved into chaos when you followed them back. Sensitive dependence on initial conditions, the fluid-dynamics people called it. As in freeway traffic, for instance, where somebody might notice a peregrine falcon resting on a light standard, and touch the brakes a moment to sustain the sight. Then the driver behind him might brake, as well, but not knowing why and slightly harder in his surprise, and so on down the miles of cars, a shock wave might build until, even if nobody collided and got killed, the traffic might tie up. The falcon, of course, would fly on. And an hour later you might pass that light pole, wondering what it was that caused the jam and looking for something big, for flashing lights, a wrecker at least, but seeing nothing.

This was fine, I thought, for traffic jams, for butterfly wings and rainstorms. That, upon examination, the whole of Western thought and even my own sense of my self had arisen from—and were conveyed upon—such delicate, transitory influences, wisps that wove this feeling of existing in the world, unsettled me a little just then.

Rock Springs

The Middle Ages didn't feel like the middle of anything. They felt like the end of days. At that point so much argued so convincingly that the conclusion was at hand, that people were living at the end of time. They lived among Roman ruins, sometimes in them, as at Arles, where they built apartments into the arches of the Coliseum. In Britain, the origins of the Roman roads were so lost in time that these engineering feats were popularly assumed to be the work of giants. Petrarch, for one, was still looking back to the Empire, when in 1341 he had himself crowned in Rome on the Capitoline, in Roman fashion with laurel, while cattle grazed on the Forum. Petrarch was convinced that he was the last liberal, the end of his line.

Ahead was the Apocalypse. The biblical omens of the end were cited often from the pulpits. The plague, the beasts of Revelations, the trumpets of doom haunted the land. All these signs were there as the close of that first millennium loomed up. But it didn't end of course, except as an abstraction, an era, afterward declared the Middle Ages, the middle, as they saw it in the eighteenth century, of that set of three: ancient, medieval, and modern.

Something new had to happen for the Middle Ages to seem to close. Eventually something new did, though just what and when is debated. Perhaps in 1150, when Aristotle's works, held in Arabic libraries, proved like ancient grain capable of germination after a winter of a thousand years. In 1323, when Aquinas was canonized and Ockham accused, something certainly began.

Then the plague years, 1347 to 1351, brought profound changes. In many places the Black Death reduced the population by half. In this period of shock, plenty, mobility, and solitude, those who had escaped the scourge of the Plague felt a strange sense of invulnerability combined with guilt. In earlier times the peasant in England had invented the playful fantasy of the Land of Cockaigne, a land of ease and plenty, where all physical needs would be instantly met, where the streams flowed with wine and chickens walked the earth roasted, with knives and forks stuck in their backs.

The aftermath of the Black Death was like some darkly ironic version of this. The survivors found the mills and farms, the furniture and tools of the dead and just took over. The shops filled with goods. In this culture of sudden riches and nameless guilt, the Church was widely perceived as corrupt, and even God, in the eyes of many, had shown no mercy, ordaining much death with little justification. So some went faithless, strangely modern, into a future weirdly enriched and depleted, the new abundance insep013-rable from the new sense of anxiety, the result of having to manage one's intentions in a universe that did not, apparently, proceed along human lines. Parades of flagellants went from town to town presenting "pageants," like medieval talk shows, that attempted to resolve the dilemma by insisting that suffering, anyway, still had meaning.

At thirty, I moved to California. My house, my job, my friends, I left behind in Illinois. A year before, I had gone to San Francisco to attend my sister's wedding, and I'd felt, in that coastal city with its hills and broad views of water, that what I'd been missing suddenly had a name. For one thing, they'd been in love, my sister and her new husband, and for another, there was that urban life, the universe of different people, not to mention the beach so nearby and all of the other California connotations promising a new life. After that trip to the wedding, it had hurt to return home, and after a year of gathering up my nerve, I headed west, driving out of town alone, on a beautiful morning in early May, too dazed to feel bereft.

What I felt was terror and exhilaration—sheer joy mingled with the sure and dreadful thought that I would never see that place or those people again. Where the interstate paralleled one runway of the Saint Louis airport, a jet was lumbering into the sky as I drove past and I noticed, beyond the runway, a cemetery. I could suddenly and vividly imagine the bones of the dead vibrating as if with eagerness as the big plane boomed just above them, packed with the living and taking off for parts unknown. After that, even the names of the Missouri towns on the exit signs seemed auspicious: Defiance, High Hill, Kingdom City, Sweet Springs, Independence. Missouri had more trees than I'd imagined, their spring canopies filling the river valleys, their color in the spring that luminous green that seems overlaid on bright yellow. "Oh my God," I kept saying aloud. "I'm doing it."

On the first night of my crossing, I slept in an old limestone hotel, the Midlands in Wilson, Kansas, a town with banners and posters advertising its Czech Festival in July. The next morning the trip felt weightier, less like a run for it, more like a long beginning. That day, amid the enormous empty landscapes of Colorado and Wyoming, I even considered changing my name. Why not? I thought. What was left of me, after this reckless, momentous, and typically American departure, all my stuff thrust into and tied on top of my tiny new Honda, like an Okie update, what was left after that probably merited a new name. Just for fun, on the long stretch as I tried to make it into Rock Springs before my exhaustion made me pull over anywhere, I searched for some hip alias, like a disc jockey's air name. Had the burden of needing a pseudonym fallen on me harder—as it does for many, crossing those mountains—I might have found one. But it was a moment's fantasy and remained such. Maybe for LA. But for San Francisco, no.

As a compromise I decided I'd be James less often in San Francisco. The formality felt vestigial, at that point. I'd be James occasionally, on my driver's license and official occasions, but for the most part I'd take my informal name and be Jim. In this way, I'd become myself more fully, I thought with my American mind. Becoming oneself was a kind of paradox, an odd endeavor with its own difficulties, but this did not occur to me then. This proved not a thought that came up much in San Francisco. In that city many people were intent on becoming themselves, wiring themselves like bonsai to maintain just that shape.

At that point, though, San Francisco lay up ahead some-where, Oz-like, farther, beyond Utah and the desert and the coast range, across the bay and into the fog. That town, ded-icated in large measure to idiosyncrasy, drew me like the promised land. In Wyoming I could gaze out at the crags of rock rising fifty miles away from the desert floor, and imag-ine that no self I could compose could be as unique, as spe-cific and obdurate as this one that coincidence—perhaps fate—had composed for me, so far.

In 1455, the printing of the Gutenberg Bible opened an age of text and closed an epoch in which most people gained in-formation through visual icons controlled by the literate few. The pages of the Gutenberg Bible itself were filled with extremely uniform letters, each Latin word composed of minims—thick, vertical marks resembling quill strokes. A reader had to work mark by mark, looking for the tenuous connectors. A word such as minimum looked like fifteen minims; millennium like seventeen.

Widespread silent reading may have arrived with print. In the early Middle Ages, text was most often sounded aloud. Saint Augustine remarks with astonishment at the rare ability of Saint Ambrose to read without speaking the words. "His eyes scanned the page, and his mind penetrated its meaning, but his voice and tongue were silent." This space within, this internal cell ringing with the text in one's own inner voice, this was new.

Bifurcated, Symmetrical, Weirdly Plural

White pants, what an idea. Still, I was traveling light that weekend, and I was going to need them. So I got them into the wash as soon as I could. On the plane I'd wadded them up, and shoved them into a side compartment of my bag. In Jess's study, I found them squashed in there and tugged them out, then had to shake the wad before it became pants again.

What was I thinking? I wondered, holding them up. I'd almost never worn them in San Francisco because they seemed semitropical, too much for the mostly muted days in the north. I couldn't even recall buying them, just then, couldn't imagine choosing them in the first place. Some whim, some clothing clerk's flattery; in any case, an aberration from the start.

For these pants, that morning's suckhole continued in

full force. They'd undoubtedly been altered, thrust into a new future. Just then, they looked tie-dyed in catsup. The tomato juice had gathered into thousands of crinkles—that chaotic stain emblematic of my difficulties on and since the airplane. But though the pants had been altered, I knew in my heart that it was my suckhole and not theirs, no matter what.

This thought somehow let me look at the pants as if I'd never seen anything like them before, and they appeared as this odd, forked object, even the term weirdly plural. Their strange, mute similarity to a human body—mine, actually, as they "fit"—clarified the whole suckhole immunity question, as I thought about it. Something had to have a mind to get caught in a suckhole—you had to be intending something else, after all, to be sidetracked. And pants were definitely dumb objects. These pants in particular looked quite dumb, even anthropomorphically idiotic.

Pants were as nothing in the intentions department, below a tree, say, which might be said to have photosynthetic intentions at least, and even seemingly below stones, which bore no clownish similarities to human beings and so might be supposed to have a life. Still, no life, no suckholes. This seemed to be a flaw in the suckhole theory. I made a mental note to tell Harry about it when I got back.

The women's laughter in the kitchen interrupted this odd thought. In the middle of hearing Les's story of her terror in the air, Jess had exclaimed "*Just* extraordinary!" Jess is a pretty, hearty woman who isn't afraid to make faces. On the ground, the tale had gotten funny, and Jess, nervous about flying herself, laughed hard at it. I took the pants out there to show them.

Steve showed me where the washer was—just around the corner, in a little alcove by the back door, which had a window onto their fenced garden. Out there bright LA morning light was falling on the dewy grass, and I felt cozy as I started the wash. I liked doing laundry. I'd done it for myself since childhood, and the various parts of the procedure comforted me, the sloshing water, the soap-smelling warmth—even the little bits, like cleaning the lint screen. It took me a long time to enjoy folding, to slow down and savor folding, but eventually that happened, too. I appreciate routine and can relish almost anything I have to do often enough.

That morning the business of washing the pants seemed especially perfect. I could let Les catch up with her friends, I could join them, chiming in through the little archway between the kitchen and the laundry room, and I had the procedure of the wash to carry me along. I located the soap and bleach, set the water level on LOW, the temperature on HOT-COLD. Taking my time with the steps, I put the soap in, put the pants in, shut the lid. I twisted the dial and pushed it in, hearing the obedient flow of the water inside the drum.

After a moment, the lid of the washer began to warm under my forearms, the long, dull, faintly bell-like sound of the jet inside ceased—the weight of the water in the tub having tripped the switch—and the humming pulse of the agitator began. Then I raised the lid again and poured a cup of limpid bleach into the soapy swishing. I looked into the steaming vat, wondering too late if it were hot water or cold that worked on tomato stains.

The pale pants rollicked around in the wash, and the washer could seem like some jiving, baptizing chapel, a minor branch of the Church of Scientific Application. It was somebody's thought process turned outward into rubber and steel and improved by teams of others, anonymous engineers and designers making science manifest, just as the anonymous stone carvers manifested the architect's plans, which manifested the bishop's order, which manifested God's will. And whoever said science wasn't spiritual, anyway? I could imagine the soul as some versatile fluid, shunted and filtered and pushed through tubes, the end spigots marked "airplane," "car," "washer," and the like.

Prosaic though it might be, practical science is to me miraculous enough. I approach technology with a folk mind, with stories. To my mind, electronics, for instance, might as well be a bee-dance down the wires, energy deciding to shuttle down one path or another, somehow expressing the ghostly will of the inventor through the motor, through the pump circulating the water, through the swish-swishing agitator, through the spinning drum. The fruits of science haven't induced in me, anyway, a scientific mind. In fact the more technology improves, the more it seems to cater to the old thought, designing in mental ergonomics, as it were, so that I can work the washer with my medieval mind.

After that, I just watched the wash rock chaotically around for a while, staring until I could reverse the motion, and make the pants truly seem to jump for joy in there, as if testifying in ecstasy, doing that dance of chaos in the wash and perfect at it somehow. More so than I ever could be, I thought idly, since the pants could just go with it, intending nothing in the first place. With that I shut the lid. Surely Jess had an ironing board around there somewhere.

The Unironic Neighbor and the Star of Dogs

In the kitchen Jess was telling a story. One of her neighbors had referred to Jessica Lange as "Jessica." Jess was a screenwriter, and her stories were usually funny and always had interesting realistic touches. Once when she and Steve were first moving into this place, she began, when the rooms were still bare of carpeting, curtains, pictures, everything, "so that it was echoey in here, without the furniture," she and her friend Tracy were hanging out in the afternoon and moving things around in the apartment, trying out arrangements and goofing on this cover story about Jessica Lange.

The story had the tone of an exposé, though there was little enough to expose. The interviewer had posed as investigative reporter—no celebrity puff piece here. She'd pressed. "You call him your husband and you're not married," she'd said.

Good grief, thought Jess, annoyed by such aggressiveness over such silliness. She exaggerated it for fun as they moved the furniture around, hooting ironically at Jessica's relations with Paco and Misha and Sam. "Just who does Jessica think she is!" said Jess, this as Margaret Dumont or somebody.

A week later when she and Steve were putting flowers in the beds in the back—it was just a mess back there when they'd moved in—a woman approached them and introduced herself as their across-the-way neighbor. Jess pointed through the wall of the kitchen as she told the story just then, to indicate the actual apartment, actually across the way.

The neighbor had just wanted to say hello and welcome. And by the way, she'd added, she couldn't disagree more about Jessica. Jessica was simply an independent woman, trying to make it in the industry, which played by men's rules. It took Jess a moment to figure out what and whom she was talking about. Evidently the neighbor had overheard Jess and Tracy camping it up in the bare, echoing rooms across the way, pretending an intimacy that the neighbor had instantly assumed true, abetted in this by her own sense of knowing Jessica Lange. Of course nobody knew anybody, Jess said.

Here in LA, the stars seemed like actual people. You even got glimpses of them in the flesh. Steve had seen Springsteen at the gym once, doing sit-ups yet, lots and lots of sit-ups. And even Steve, who doesn't approve of this kind of thing, had to say hello and introduce himself. Jess encouraged him to say it, actually, knowing that he wanted to.

Steve had told Springsteen that he'd heard him perform "Pretty Flamingo" once, in a club on Sunset, and Bruce, a regular guy, very friendly, had replied that he liked that song, but had for some reason never recorded it. Steve thanked him. "Nice talking to you," he said. "Same here," said Bruce, going back to his sit-ups.

I could understand why the unironic neighbor felt she could speak in Jessica Lange's defense. You felt that you knew the stars, though they did not know you. They were rich and isolated, though you might glimpse them. Their nearness was one of the attractive things about LA, but—I could already tell—might become one of its long-term pains. Here you stood in their direct radiance, and up close you might get singed. In the Middle Ages, at least the saints weren't driving around town in great cars and working on their abs.

You could camp up the whole star thing, but you couldn't live in Hollywood without feeling its effect, unless you were a bodhisattva or a pure dork. It was as if there were no shade in that bright hierarchy, no dimness in which to cast your own faint light. I knew I'd be subject to this too, if I lived here. Being a bodhisattva seemed out of the question, and I knew I wasn't a pure dork, either. For one thing, I recalled the moment on the plane when I had decided not to dress like one.

The washer was spinning its tub by now, but no longer making those intermittent jetting noises indicative of the rinse cycle. Soon it would click off altogether and drop the damp pants into the cool, speckled enamel chamber, finally still. About this time Steve proposed that we go to brunch—it would have to be lunch, he said, if we hung out any longer. As usual, Steve made things happen. At his suggestion we broke up to get our stuff, Les and I returning to our room to rummage in the luggage.

"I can't change," I said.

"Everyone wears shorts down here," she said.

Before I went out, I found that the washer had stopped, and having no time to check them, I just flopped the wet pants into the dryer, set it for an hour, and pressed the button. The dryer rumbled to something like life. Then we all left the house, donning shades against the brightness and intent on finding some food.

*L*ater, remembering the story about Jessica Lange and feeling because of it that I also knew her, I read with interest another interview with her in *TV Guide*. In it she told a story about walking her dogs at night in the country in Minnesota, where she grew up. It had snowed all day that day, but after dark the stars had come out, and Jessica Lange left the last warm light of home behind and proceeded across the meadow, the snow silvery under the moon. The dogs, wild to be out at night, barked and raced through the soft snow banks around the old logging trail. The sky was awake with galaxies and looked like some dark celestial reef. Jessica herself wore a hooded white cape. Her breath made clouds in the cold air.

She liked to lie down in the snow sometimes, she'd confessed to the interviewer. So when the dogs got out ahead of her in the meadow, she picked her spot and lay down in the soft snow. As usual one dog, the most vigilant, noticed that she had disappeared. The others caught his anxiety and followed him as he began to look for her in the drifts. Silent, steaming, almost invisible in her white cape, she lay there under the stars, Jessica Lange, the movie star, the actual person who was telling the story. Then one by one, the dogs, circling and sniffing, discovered her. As at a signal, they sat down around her in the snow, forming a star of dogs, surveying the meadow and starting to guard.

The Allegory of the Shades

Harry hated sunglasses, even ordinary shades like the Wayfarers I was wearing in LA that weekend. He hated the dimming down of it all, he'd said. I, who could wear shades, was just not visual.

I had another, fancier pair of sunglasses, which made things look gold, but I'd left them at home. Those I'd gotten for skiing, something I rarely did, though they'd proved useful anyway in San Francisco, where the gold lenses warmed the white days of summer, when the fog dissolved the hills. I'd never gotten used to that cool, white light in July, and these old skiing sunglasses made things seem summerish to me. But LA was burnished enough, poured over with desert sun and needing some cooling shade, not gold lenses.

Besides, I'd be hanging out with other people in LA, and

the gold glasses were mirrored. I didn't feel fit for society in mirrored shades. The mirroring might have some good effect on the slopes—who knew what?—but in company I felt I should show my eyes, which seemed sincere and fair. I'd conducted conversations with people in mirrored shades myself, and had been forced to watch my own image—seeing what *they* saw rather than seeing them see me—as we talked. Mirrored shades were disconcerting. So for the sake of others—namely Les, who hated those mirrored gold glasses—I'd left them at home.

On the sidewalk I put on my Wayfarers, conventional sunglasses with that square romantic name reminiscent of wandering Odysseus and of Burl Ives singing "I'm just a poor wayfarin' stranger, travelin' through this world of woe," with that guitar of his plunking along, back in the fifties, when such a tune could count for the blues. The gray-green tint of the Wayfarers was a businesslike substitute for the brightness, a balm; to wear them was to step innocently, functionally, almost medicinally into a portable shade, a tiny patch of it that seemed to cool down all of broad, hot LA.

No matter which shades I wore, though, I knew I would notice them only momentarily. This was the rule with shades. Whether things were golder or bluer or greener, whether the frames themselves stood in the field of vision or not, shades became ubiquitous and, like all constants, disappeared. Nobody went around in shades saying, "Things only *look* like this."

That was why Harry hated sunglasses. He had a firmer sense than I did that his own perspective was the real one. He couldn't believe in the way things looked through sunglasses, and he knew that once he'd worn them for a while, he'd have to. Once he'd tried on my gold glasses and had ripped them off his face in disgust. "*This* is how things look to you?" he'd said. "How can you wear these? It's a dream world in there."

Glare, he thought, was preferable. Of course he wore glasses himself, round, untinted prescription lenses, but he wore those all the time, so they didn't count.

I'm Like I'm Sure

It all took time. The Commandments had to be dictated, also subsidiary directions of all kinds: the description of the ark and tabernacle, of the garments and jewels of the high priests. The width of the court of the Holy of Holies was prescribed and the clarity of the lamp oil, the proportions of spices and frankincense in the holy perfume. The elaborations went on and on.

In the wilderness down below, the people couldn't know all this, of course. To them, it had simply been too long. How soon they had forgotten, these obstinate people, disregarding the plagues cast upon their captors, even the parting of the fluid sea. They needed a god and they needed one now. They went to Aaron—the mouthpiece, whose eloquence even God had praised—and asked him to make a new god for them, one that might guide them through the desert.

So even as God was describing the golden breastplate, the checkered tunic, the turban and sash, and robe of blue and violet and scarlet that this same Aaron would wear before the multitude, Aaron was conceiving a golden work on his own. In *The Ten Commandments* it is the Edward G. Robinson character, the heavy, who incites the treachery, though in the Bible, which has more emotion, more complexity, more historical ungainliness, it is Aaron, a good man essentially and the brother of Moses.

"Tear the gold rings from the ears of your wives, of your sons and daughters, and bring them to me," Aaron said. He had these melted in a crucible and poured into a mold. Broken free, the gold resembled a cow. They put this golden calf on an altar and burnt offerings to it, saying, "This is your god, O Israel."

For anyone following the text, this act is deeply ironic, for what has God just prohibited—twenty pages earlier—and prohibited first and foremost, before false witness or adultery or theft or murder? His first commandments: "You shall make no other gods before Me. You shall not make for yourself an idol." In the movie the irony is heavy handed, accomplished in jump cuts from the calf to Moses wincing on the mountain as God, a flaming whirlwind, inscribes just these commandments into the rock.

Steve drove. Handsome, capable Steve was the master of logistics, especially in LA, where he worked as a line producer for CNN. He had anchorman qualities, Steve, and though I had a pang at seeing the Pontiac I had rented remain at the curb, I was happy to relinquish to him the trouble of negotiating the traffic.

The street they lived on ran across the big boulevards: Sunset, Wilshire, Santa Monica, Melrose. Steve drove south, across Melrose toward Beverly. These boulevards had mile after mile of strip malls, store after store—some of them nice, with Il Fornaio trucks double-parked out front— but most ordinary, somebody's idea of filling a market niche, taco places and Shoe Cities and hundreds of yogurt shops, with *yogurt* spelled in all kinds of ways. *Yogart* was popular. Yogurt stores said a lot about LA, I decided, about the dread of fat and the need to be consoled by some trivial sweetness. We'll find our way out of this somehow, they seemed to say.

Here and there, above the streets, the same pink billboard advertised someone named Angelyne, a platinum blonde, semirecumbent, peering over the tops of her heart-shaped shades, her enormous breasts withheld by strong black webbing which, blown up to that size, looked like cargo nets. What was her deal, this Angelyne? What could she possibly get back from her huge advertising expenditure? Did she jump out of a cake at stag parties? Did she model jewelry on the shopping channel? Or did she just spend the money to see her image huge over Melrose Avenue, having worked so hard to exaggerate it?

It turned out that Jess had actually seen Angelyne in Hollywood, in the grocery store parking lot it turned out. She'd been driving a pink Corvette, wearing a leopard-skin skirt, accompanied by her young, long-haired, rocker boyfriend. Angelyne advertised herself for movie roles,

Jess said. She'd had some success with it, even. She'd gotten the attention of John Waters, for one thing, and had been in a couple of his movies: *Hairspray* or *Polyester*. Said Jess, "Waters probably came out here from Baltimore, took one look at that billboard, and said, 'I *have* to have her in my movie.' But then he would—he's so camp."

On the mountaintop God noticed the golden calf business immediately, of course, and was furious about the people burning offerings to this image of a cow. Moses had to plead with God to dissuade him from burning *them*, then and there. "Change thy mind," Moses asked, and God did, for the moment, sending the prophet back down to deal with his short-sighted people and giving him two stone tablets loaded with preliminary instructions, these to shatter in their faces, just to show them.

These tablets weren't smashed in the movie. They were saved and eventually sold at auction at Christie's. According to *Buzz* magazine, they were made of fiberglass and were inscribed with the words, "Honor thy father and mother and place your right foot on the adhesive tape X."

We went for brunch to a café called Revival and sat at a sidewalk table under a white canvas umbrella off the busy avenue called La Brea—the tar pits weren't far away. I sat facing the broad street and watching the pedestrians make their slow progress across the enormous intersection at Beverly, lanes and lanes on all sides. Beneath outsized, Saul

Steinbergesque objects, the walkers plied the hot flat expanses, their progress so minuscule behind the traffic that it was hard to watch them patiently, as they made their way across the intersection and down the sidewalk toward the Beverly Plaza strip mall, which had an Egghead Software and a Toppers Yogurt. From where I sat I had to watch these pedestrians labor beneath a gigantic billboard, its single brown support thicker than an oil drum and thirty feet high, holding up a picture of a gargantuan Chevrolet and the huge words "Personal Space."

Descending the mountain with his dictation unfinished, Moses heard the people singing in the camp. Down there they were dancing wildly. In the movie, it's all very Isadora Duncan, with bellowing timpani and orgy grapes and flowing garlands, even a sacrificial virgin and nudity mentioned in the voice-over though not shown on the screen. In the Bible, Moses burst into their party in a rage and snatched up the golden calf. He burned it and ground it to powder and threw the powder in water and made them drink it. And brother Aaron, suddenly not so eloquent, could only stutter out this lame excuse: "I threw the gold into the fire," he said, "and out came this calf." Duh.

Moses then went to the camp's gate and called his supporters to him—the Lord's people, they are called. Moses bid them to kill the reprobates—"every man his brother, every man his friend, every man his neighbor." And though they killed some three thousand, Yahweh was not assuaged.

"Leave this place," God commanded then, adding that he wouldn't be going with them. "Should I go up in your midst for one moment," He said, "I would destroy you." So he withdrew his presence.

In the kabalistic tradition, such withdrawal is God's archetypal action. Called zimzum, it occurs at the first moment, when God withdraws himself to produce the vacuum in which creation itself may occur.

We ordered brunch—Les got a little pizza with zucchini, yellow squash, and garlic. For me, still in breakfast mode, a frittata with home fries; for Jess and Steve their usuals at this café: focaccia sandwiches, mozzarella and eggplant and honey-baked ham with fontina, respectively. We sat there under the white umbrella waiting for our food to arrive. A guy at the table across from me looked like a pirate, with his earring and his bandanna tight across his shaved head. His girlfriend wore black combat boots—punk women always seem so well prepared to me—and the two joked about having to do the voice-over for an orgasm scene. On the street maybe a hundred cars a minute went by, as the tiny walkers, in groups of two and three, continued to pass.

There was something unusual about these pedestrians, I noticed. The women wore long skirts, the men wore black suits and white shirts and ties and yarmulkes, but they were all wearing the same kind of shoes. They were wearing ancient garb and sneakers.

The food came, with huge goblets of coffee. At a nearby table, a man in purple shorts—like mine—ate his brunch as his boxer, on a leash beneath the table, calmly licked his master's knee. The man had on sneakers, too—huge, new, black-and-white Nike basketball shoes. The passing Hasidim wore plain sneakers, though occasionally there was a fancier pair—like plaid Converse high-tops worn by one little girl—but still, canvas sneakers, not massive, heathen sneakers like the guy at the table with his dog.

I pointed these shoes out to my friend Les and she didn't want to look, as she is Jewish herself and felt a little guilty. They're fasting today, she said, looking at her pizzetta. And not driving, either. And evidently, I thought, not wearing leather on the Day of Atonement.

Near our table, two older Jewish men, bearded, one in a yarmulke, one in a dark-brimmed hat and a white silk cape, both in white sneakers, passed silently, seemingly unnoticed by anyone but me, like ancient figures revisiting this place, shades in Keds.

Until his third trip to the mountain, Moses was unable to soothe God's rage. At last, though, they struck the bargain that gave his people a future as a nation and that required, among other things, that they atone forever for their sin of idolatry, humbling themselves each year on the tenth day of the seventh month—Yom Kippur—and meditating on the one true God.

"Humble your souls," God prescribed for that day, "and present an offering by fire to the Lord."

The synagogue was right next door. It was called Kollel, and in the rare pauses in the passing traffic, I could hear the cantor pitching just a note or two of his song. At the neighboring table, a woman said, "And I was like 'Yeah!' and she was like 'There are stars coming in here all the time, like what's her name, the one who used to be on *Night Court*.'"

Three young boys, brothers maybe, went past, the littlest one hanging on the middle one familiarly, and all three in baggy suits, leaning into one another with the same calm intimacy shown by the rest of these Hasidic passersby. It was a solemn day, but the burden of atonement fell upon everyone alike, and so they could take some consolation in the company.

At a nearby table the guy in the bandanna said, "He said, 'She looks like Madonna but prettier, kind of Bambi eyes, you know, really sexy and really innocent.'" Said the woman in the boots, "I'm like I'm sure."

The people shall afflict themselves on Yom Kippur—this came from Leviticus, that book subtitled "The Law of Burnt Offerings," which delineated the commandments of purity, detailing bathing rituals, times of sexual abstinence, the stoning of necromancers, and the like. The particular Yom Kippur afflictions had to be codified a millennium later, with Jerusalem destroyed and the religion having to be made portable for the long wandering ahead. So the rabbis authorized five particular afflictions for the Day of Atonement: neither eat nor drink, nor have sexual relations, nor bathe, nor go forth shod. A thousand years later, this last prohibition against shoes probably proved a greater hardship in the shtetls of Russia than had been intended back in temperate Palestine. At some point No Shoes had moderated to No Leather Shoes, and after another thousand years, on Beverly Boulevard in LA in America on that particular day, had come to Keds, in which one was still, apparently, not quite shod.

Jess and Les noticed a man at another table who was Hollywood handsome and who was wearing a tattered felt cowboy hat. Steve and I, put off by the women's ogling, made fun of him. "His mule must have bitten that hole in his hat," said Steve. Then we noticed he had on blue-and-yellow cross-country skiing shoes, with those long tabs sticking out in front. These provided us with all the evidence we needed, though Jess teased us, saying, "I don't know—I think you guys might be wearing those next year." It was odd to think of foot fashion at that moment, of this guy in the hat striving to ignite a cross-country skiing shoe fad. Still, there was no telling what people might wear.

The sneakers worn by Hasidim on Yom Kippur couldn't be considered a fashion statement, I thought idly. They *meant* something, for one thing. What fashion promised had to go unnamed, except by the name fashionable, an infinite regress. Not knowing why was an important part of fashion, letting you embrace whatever it was as the ever-changing embodiment of ineffable coolness, that which always seemed to depart just as I arrived, showing up at the party in my cross-country skiing shoes.

How odd it seemed, just then, for it to be possible to be profane at this point in the twentieth century, and odder still to consider that it remained possible to put on sacredness. I ate my breakfast and made small talk with my friends, considering the possibility of cleaving to some exacting way of proceeding that canceled all the vagaries, that let some pure intention—God's intention—purify you and all the objects in your life. And which was, besides that, actual, manifested in the ordinary things of the moment, footwear, for instance.

When from the blazing bush God first commanded Moses, Moses could only doubt his own capacities and answer, "Who am I, that I should go to Pharaoh?" Only later did Moses think to ask who God was. When charged with leading the people out of fleshpot Egypt, he anticipates trying to convince them. "Now they may say to me," Moses said to God, "'what is His name?'" And God, whom no one had ever named or ever would, answered, "I am who I am," this *name* rendered in the text as YHWH, the unpronounceable tetragrammaton, derived from a verb—*hayah*, to be.

Maybe I was being too hard on this guy in his tattered hat, I thought. Maybe he just liked his cross-country skiing shoes. Maybe they reminded him of his boyhood back in crisp and snowy Minnesota. Then, looking at the shoes themselves, with their munchkin colors, I thought, nah.

Atom and Void

S̶ome fifty years after George Berke-
ley refuted the existence of matter, James Boswell embarked
on a journey from England to the continent. His friend Dr.
Johnson accompanied him as far as Harwich, where they se-
cured Boswell's passage by packet boat. They dined at an inn
near the docks, and during dinner Boswell happened to remark that he hoped Johnson would return soon to London.
It would be terrible, Boswell said, if the Doctor should have
to remain long in so dull a place as Harwich.

The Doctor, who disliked the use of words of dispro-
portionate magnitude—one didn't *discuss* a pimple, for
instance—rebuked Boswell. "It would not be *terrible*," he
said, if he were so detained.

After eating they went next door to the church and approached the altar. Johnson made Boswell pray. He sent

Boswell to his knees, saying, "Now that you are going to leave your native country, recommend yourself to the protection of your CREATOR and REDEEMER." Johnson's piety, writes Boswell, was "constant and fervent."

Then, emerging from the church, they spoke about Bishop Berkeley, of his "ingenious sophistry to prove the non-existence of matter." Boswell remarked that, though they were satisfied that the doctrine was not true, it was impossible to refute. Instantly, and with "mighty force," Johnson kicked a large stone, answering, as he bounced off it, "I refute it *thus.*"

Boswell was impressed, though he still could not conceive how Berkeley's refutation could be answered with pure reasoning. He was sure, though, that had not politics turned Dr. Johnson aside from "calm philosophy," he would surely have undertaken "this nice and difficult task."

It's easy to forget that the Church's condemnation of Galileo and the publication of Descartes's *Discourse on Method* were roughly concurrent events—the mind, mine anyway, wants a millennium between. In fact, there were just four years, between 1633 and 1637. And so briefly later, the eighteenth century had begun, by which time the establishment of modernity had already proceeded a long way. By then Pascal had passed through his night of the soul and Newton had published his *Principia.* Most recently, John Locke had ascribed all mental ideas to sensory input, arguing that nothing in the mind came from anywhere but the world, that we began blank and became inscribed by our days.

To reasonable men of the time, this seemed a sound concept. Locke had grounded his formulations in a conception of physical matter that appeared undeniable. "Who doubts matter doth but dream he makes the question," he wrote. Enter the Bishop Berkeley, dreaming his irrefutable dream.

Locke's matter was composed of corpuscles, in a universe of hopeful mechanics called Corpuscularianism, which reached back to the ancient Greek Democritus for its atomic theories. The concept of freely moving atoms in a neutral and infinite space had provided the basis for verifying Copernican theory and for Newton's establishment of gravity as a universal force.

One remaining problem with atoms, though, was that one still had to decide which phenomena arose from their interaction and which arose from our perception of that interaction. These perceptions were appearances only, according to Democritus. "Hot and cold are appearance," he had written. "Sweet and bitter are appearance, color is appearance—in reality there are the atoms and the void."

To the conservative Irish Bishop Berkeley—to whom Newton was "a philosopher of a neighboring nation"—this modern, materialistic, atomic theory was the Font of Error. God, not piles of atoms, manifested the nature of things. By then great forces—no less than the course of Western history—were arrayed against this view, and challenging them was no easy matter. Matter, indeed, was the matter. This fundamental modern concept Berkeley set out to refute. To disprove it, he took up the rigorous, logical methods respected by his opponents, what Boswell refers to as "pure reasoning." That one's opponent's methods *are* one's opponent apparently did not occur to him.

Berkeley chose to aggravate that little problem with the modern mind, that small nag from the time of Democritus about atoms and perception, appearances and reality. Locke himself had acknowledged that matter possessed certain characteristics that we might call "subjective." These "secondary" characteristics were as the hum of the recorder, features of the sensing device, not what was sensed. Things had "primary" characteristics as well, luckily enough, and the study of these might disregard such perceptual niceties.

Berkeley contested this distinction. By empirical critique he greatly encroached upon the grounds of objectivity, demonstrating the difficulty of divorcing any object from its perceiving subject. Speaking empirically, he asserted that no way could exist to withhold some qualities of reality as more real, even those more observable and quantifiable qualities.

Finally and devastatingly, Berkeley refuted the empirical conception of matter itself. Matter as the empiricists defined it was "an unknown somewhat," he wrote, demonstrating that rational analysis could not ultimately prove the existence of any matter outside the mind. So Berkeley sought to close off the possibilities for the existence of an objective, empirical universe. To his spiritual heirs, Berkeley's argument would prove vexingly airtight.

For Berkeley's victory, too, was ironic. The bishop had not intended, after all, to uphold individual subjectivity as the basis for reality, but, in the spirit of Ockham, to reinstate God's subjectivity as that basis. In the universe as Berkeley saw it, to be was to exist in the mind of God. The world was God's thought. Shared perceptions—that a violet to you was a violet to me—arose because humanity perceived with and was perceived by God's mind, in which violets had that purple, smelled that way. And this was where we'd go, back to paradise. So Berkeley assumed as he strove to stem the modern tide.

It didn't quite work out that way, or hasn't so far, anyway. Berkeley's argument managed instead to liberate the thing, to give the modern ideas he opposed an independent existence. Like Ockham, Berkeley's true and lasting contribution was his demonstration of the power of the new method to explode previous assumption. His extreme argument would prove extremely useful to his opponent, David Hume, who would borrow from the bishop's tools what he needed, and employ this improved method to empty the Lockean universe of its verities.

There would be no rock to kick, and no foot. Matter wanted rational justification, as Berkeley had argued. But so did God, in whom even such as Locke had invested cause. Following Berkeley, Hume could undermine as well the ultimate rational assumption, that a mind existed to do the assuming. So, instead of turning the West back to Eden, to the mind and God in mutual contemplation, Berkeley unwittingly and potently assisted the modern moment, accelerating it, even, hastening the slide. Thus the West would pass as through some vortex into this ungainly new universe, a cosmos still contingent upon signs—rife with them, even—though of what we'd each now have to decide.

Seventeen years after Johnson kicked the stone outside the church door in Harwich, he found himself again in a circumstance of farewell, and in that instance again referred to Berkeley. At home in London, Johnson bid good-bye to a gentleman of Berkeley's persuasion and was recorded as adding, wittily, "Pray, Sir, don't leave us; for we may perhaps forget to think of you, and then you will cease to exist."

Something similar may have entered Boswell's mind as well, when he said good-bye to his friend in Harwich that day seventeen years before. After Johnson kicked the stone, he and Boswell walked the beach for a time, spending a last few moments together. At last they embraced and promised to correspond, pledging also not to forget each other in this period of absence. "It is more likely you should forget me," said Johnson.

Finally they had to part, and Boswell got aboard his boat. As it pulled into the open sea, he watched at the railing as Johnson stood watching on the shore. Each was much moved at the farewell, and perhaps it had been, after all, Boswell's impending departure that lent such vehemence to Johnson's insistence on the existence of matter. The immateriality that had bothered Johnson most, in other words, was the potential absence of his friend. For what does matter matter, really, if not for this?

From the railing, Boswell watched the beach recede, the Doctor's "majestic frame" diminish in the distance. Johnson was the first to turn away, from his view of the ship on the water, his friend by then tiny at the rail. Johnson's eyesight was worse, after all. "At last I perceived him walk back into the town," wrote the waterborne Boswell, "and he disappeared."

Still Unfinished Xanadu

After brunch we went downtown, all the way on surface streets, mostly on Beverly Boulevard, through Korea Town and another area still riot torn, as the newscasters say, the burnt stuff still in evidence, past a broad tropical park with a pond, around which a crowd of men seemed to be waiting for something, maybe for work.

Then we surmounted a little hill and entered downtown. Steve was pointing out the *LA Law* tower, now another TV icon as well as a place of work, and as I looked up, I happened to see an airplane crossing the sky. That was me, I thought. That plane was where I had been, just hours earlier. I'd actually been up there in the sky. The controlled, unreal environment of the airplane hadn't been a dream or a story or a commercial or some sort of elaborate simulation, but had been there, in an actual space in the air at what had been the present moment. Les had gripped my arm and I'd looked out of the window as the plane had banked, gazing into the canyons of downtown, through which I was now passing at this present moment, in a tiny car among the buildings that had seemed like somebody's collection. For a moment, it impressed me. Then, even an instant later in the moving car, buildings obscured the vista and the airplane was gone, and that firm sense had evaporated, leaving a strangeness I could recall but no longer feel, which was gradually replaced with a little self-rebuke. Of course, what could be more obvious than that?

By then Steve was pointing out the new library, a sort of Babylonian structure, just rebuilt since the big fire, which had destroyed three hundred thousand volumes. I thought of Louise then, who had recently had an interview for the job of performance director at the LA library. I recalled also the burning of the library called the Sarapeum in Alexandria in 391 A.D. And the unending period afterward in which people weren't influenced by books that had ceased to exist.

From the gravel parking lot on another hilltop, we climbed a steel staircase to an upper street. Steve pointed out the Music Center in the distance and beyond that an office tower resembling a cooling stack. Downtown compounded that strong, strange presence of LA I'd felt on Beverly Boulevard, of discrete, huge objects and the few tiny pedestrians beneath them lending vast scale to that space, like a few antelope among mesas. In the middle of the broad street, I could look through the traffic island to another street beneath. The whole hill seemed layered with roadway.

In a garden between high-rises, we found a long, still, raised pool, the water pouring evenly off its edges in one smooth sheet. On that windless day, the pool was so still that any little impulse made it seem electric and awake. I plunked my hand in the water. The rounded trough focused the colliding rings into bands of waves that ran in stately parallels up the whole length—maybe thirty yards—between rows of potted magnolias. The glass towers overhead made a gridded reflection, which the tiny waves, seeming to condense as they receded, set into intricate vibration.

Steve splashed the water again, and sent a second set of waves after the first, and when these two collided—the first on its way back already—the reflections were charged for a moment with the tremulous, weirdly regular static of their interference pattern, which resolved as the two sets passed through each other and parted. Steve and I watched this for a time, as the women walked ahead. The surface seemed to approach stillness forever, though, and eventually we couldn't wait.

Then, coincidentally enough, Steve took us to an overpass where we could see one of Lloyd's sculptures. We looked down into the next layer and there was Lloyd's piece. I'd completely forgotten that Steve and Jess had met Louise and Lloyd. We'd all had martinis together at the Shangri-la once, on a previous trip when I barely knew Jess and Steve. Steve had taken an interest in Lloyd's work then, and had realized that he had actually seen one of Lloyd's sculptures—this piece—every day from the window of his office when he worked in a law firm downtown.

The work was a big concrete rocker with life-sized, color-ful, cut-out cars in primary colors atop it. Posed there beside actual speeding cars on the roadway, the sculpture beamed, turning the traffic into something rollicking and bright and making the whole business of downtown seem happy and silly and lucky.

It made me miss Lloyd to see the sculpture. Too bad I wouldn't be seeing him. Lloyd was probably in his studio at that moment out there in the flat warehouse district west of the skyscrapers. The last time I'd been there, Lloyd had spoken Spanish on the phone to one of his suppliers. The place had smelled of sawdust.

Lloyd had lived in LA almost all of his life, having come here from San Francisco as a toddler. As a child Lloyd had witnessed VJ Day on Hollywood Boulevard, he'd told me once. He'd been astonished at the crowds of grown-ups shouting and embracing. Then as a precocious high school art student, he had been sent to a class at Chouinard, where he was confronted for the first time with a female model in the nude. At the time, he hadn't been able to maintain his composure in the presence of such powerful nakedness, he'd said. He'd had to flee the room.

The Shimmer

J

ohn Cage was valedictorian of his
class at LA High. He went on to Pomona in 1928, where he
was shocked to see so many of his college classmates reading the same assigned book. For his part, he went into the
library and read the first book he found by an author
whose last name began with Z. When, after this exercise,
he still got the highest grade in the class, he dropped out of
college.

That day I didn't know why, exactly, I'd wanted to see the
Cage show. Maybe there was some other reason, but mostly
the show was what happened to be at the Museum of Contemporary Art. Afterward, when I began to have the odd

feeling that the weekend was fated, this show, a various and extravagant exhibition with a Joycean name—*Rolywholy-over*—seemed perfect, suspiciously so. At the time, though, I was just going there to go there. We descended beneath the glass pyramids that pierce the roof plane of MOCA, their sarcophagal quality reminding me involuntarily of Indiana Jones.

Cage I didn't know about. I thought of him as a composer, famous for his silent compositions. These didn't seem too promising, for a museum show. But when I looked at the list of artists on the written guide, I saw that it wasn't just Cage's work in the show. The brochure listed hundreds of artists, among them Duchamp, Rauschenberg, Beuys, even Yoko Ono. Looking at the list more closely, I noticed the Marx brothers, too.

Inside it was hard not to feel disoriented. The big room was jammed with objects, with Plexiglas cases on wheels and rolling carts full of stuff and paintings crowding the walls, some of them hanging so high up that they were difficult to see. The gallery technicians seemed to be still working on the exhibition. Two of them moved through the Saturday crowd carting a big canvas, a Jasper Johns painting of the US map, the states stenciled with abbreviations for their names—NEB, IND, FLA, MO.

The work jostled past us. Slate gray obliterated many of the defining colors and features of the states, though I could still tell that it was a map. That was the sixties idea, the sign disjointed from what it signified, though just enough to make the combination shimmer a little conceptually. The art part—the paint, whatever wasn't the sign—acted on the other as a kind of built-in accident, and that shimmer was the interference between the two.

Cage's father invented a high-powered airplane engine in 1918—an exploding one, at that. It blew up on the ground, at any rate. The alloys needed to contain such power had not yet been invented, though by then something like them had been proven necessary. Cage's father gave him this advice in life. "If someone says *can't*," he said, "that shows you what to do." Off went Cage, no way wrong.

The whole show shimmered like that, between what was intended and what wasn't. Cage had organized—or disorganized—the exhibition, treating it as he had his musical compositions. In a corner, a bank of computers generated chance operations (earlier in his career, Cage had simply thrown the *I Ching*), and these random results determined the placement and duration of the artworks in the display. That's why the technicians were moving the work around, so that the display would be, as Cage had said of his music, "something like the weather." A circus, he called the show. Certainly it circulated. It made me a little uncomfortable actually. For one thing, I couldn't see the whole show. What I saw, I saw only in its momentary aspect. Usually art seemed to solve this problem.

Once a student had told me that her favorite art was the clouds, and I hadn't been able to convince her that clouds aren't art. Nobody makes clouds, I'd said. God makes clouds, she'd said. It had been frustrating. This show gave me that feeling. I wished they would just put all the paintings on the wall and let me look.

On the gallery floor sat big, transparent Plexiglas cases with drawers full of letters and feathers and rocks and odd musical scores that looked like electronic schematics. One manuscript turned out to be field notes by Henry Thoreau. The nineteenth-century anarchist's slanted, quickly composed handwriting was insistent yet not quite legible. Notes to himself, they looked like. Right in the middle of the text he'd sketched a stem and a leaf and what could have been a waterbug. At the top I could make out only the world *remarkably*. Nearby was one of Cage's own letters, neatly typewritten and definitely to someone, quoting Thoreau. "Drawing anything conveys it indelibly to the memory," it said.

On the wall nearby and across the entire twentieth century was a drawing, pencil on canvas, by Tom Marioni, a series of thick, vertical pencil lines, all about a foot long, drawn more or less atop one another until they'd become a bunch about an inch wide. It was called *Drawing a Line as Far as I Can Reach*. The marks seemed to bear only the slightest relation to anyone's intentions, like the more or less accidental by-product of some quasi-mechanical process.

As a young composer, Cage had gone to the anechoic chamber at Harvard, to hear true silence. There, if anywhere, he thought he'd find it. Spongy buffers, curtain after curtain, filtered out all incoming sound waves. But there was no silence in the anechoic chamber. In that quiet, Cage found himself instead aware suddenly of his body's own music, the tiny flick of his blinking, the gurgle of his guts, his two-toned heartbeat, even the rush of his blood through the veins of his ears. What he'd called silence was relative. Its experience included the hum and pulse of the mechanism, that and whatever else we chose not to hear. You could say that Cage did hear silence in the anechoic chamber, and found it full of sound. In any case, he left feeling more flexible about pauses in his music. After that, his work became "an exploration of nonintention," he said.

About this time, I ran into someone from San Francisco, a publicist whom I barely knew, and just because he was from San Francisco—and so in this context a comrade—I said hello. A mistake. He took off talking and didn't stop, dropping about four names a minute, lacing a few of his clients' names among those of the art stars. Meantime my friends took off. Les pointed at Jess, then at herself, then pointed up, indicating that she and Jess were ascending somewhere. Steve had already been shunted off into the circulating art.

When I finally disengaged myself from the guy, I wandered into a section of the show in which some twenty museums, all within a thirty-mile radius of MOCA, had contributed various objects selected at random. The LA Children's Museum, the Cabrillo Marine Museum, and the Museum of Jurassic Technology, among others, had sent things. A glass display case some ten feet up on the wall was said to contain an intricately carved almond stone. Also displayed here were four manhole covers, a French peep show, circa 1820, the skull of a small elephant seal, a photo of the

Utopians of LA at their annual ball, a Dali necktie, and, from Frederick's of Hollywood, the cream-colored bustier worn by Ingrid Bergman in *Cactus Flower*.

$\mathfrak{C}$age wrote that anything resembling an interruption or distraction should be welcomed. "By these interruptions and distractions and flexibilities" he said, "we enrich the brushing of information against information."

$\mathcal{A}$ woman asked me for help. She didn't get this show, she said. I told her that she only thought she didn't get it. "Just be with it a while," I said, as if I were. "It changes all the time." I pointed her to a piece I'd seen before, the famous erased de Kooning. It was a drawing that his friend had erased, I said. Was it valuable? she asked, and when I told her it was, she said, "That's mean." It was a Zen thing, I offered. She seemed unhelped by this, though she wandered off in the direction of the piece.

Another woman, who'd witnessed this exchange, came over to me, her girlfriend hovering some twenty yards off. She didn't understand all this, she said. "What about that one, for instance?" She pointed to a Rauschenberg painting across the gallery and about fifteen feet up on the wall. The painting was mostly black, and had a lot of stuff combined in it, including a man's tie and the partially obliterated word *King*. I had nothing to offer this woman. What am I, a guide? I thought. Why me? I could almost feel myself shimmering, giving off some aura or vibration that made me appear to belong there in that chaotic and odd exhibition.

Cage distrusted harmony. Percussion he liked. Percussion isn't open ended, he believed—it's just open. It doesn't even promise to end. His percussion piece *Four*[4] was very spare —Cage himself said of it that it was hard for trained performers to do so little. Its first performance took place in the Sculpture Garden of the Museum of Modern Art in New York on a summer evening in 1991, just months before Cage himself died. That night ambient, unintended sounds filled the outdoor venue: the unending rumble of traffic, which Cage enjoyed and compared to the sea; near and distant car honk and brake squeal; tires flapping over pavement joints; buses grinding bassily away; also taxi whistles, unintelligible shouts, and the occasional clop of city heels on the avenue.

All this was included in the performance, framed by the minimal percussion from the players. There was also some "real" music. That night in the midst of the performance of Cage's piece, there arose from the streets beyond the museum a repeated tune from a saxophone, played—badly, though this distinction lacked meaning in that context—by some guy for pocket change.

Out there in the city night, these sounds reverberated, climbed the straight stone faces, disappeared into the upper stories. The audience took it in, if they could, the occasional percussion acting as a kind of homing beacon, from which they might range out among these other sounds, experience the brushing of information against information, and return, having heard the music that was always there, whether it was called silence or not. "You Won't Hear Anything," said an announcement for a Cage concert; "You'll Hear Everything."

Sensible

Everything was too much, by then, and I had to flee the exhibition. I searched for Les and Jess and found them looking at stuff in the museum shop. There I bought the mirrored box containing the loose-leaf catalogue for the show, thinking that at least I'd have it in one container. Then the three of us found Steve, who'd been scouting and now had something else to show.

He led us back across the roof of the museum, then down into a sunken plaza, where there was an elaborate fountain in an amphitheater that had pools for stages. In and around these pools a set of mechanical geysers was performing, dozens of jets going off in a prolonged dance, a waterclock ballet. It was a relief then to watch fluid having to conform, choreographed to shoot and splatter, to froth and stagleap and hold itself aloft on cue.

We had arrived in midsequence and so had to wait through the ending to see the whole thing. The display had a big finish. A cascade poured down the steps toward the spectators and, at the last minute, was magically drawn off. Then the pools drained, the fountain reset its hydraulic process, and the show began again.

I felt sheepishly grateful for this fountain, after Cage, and let myself be coddled by its Magic Kingdomish spectacle, glad to put aside my vigilance toward the actualities, heliocentric or otherwise. I just watched the water, wondering whether I really wanted to relinquish the old sense of things, my medieval mind.

I was fond of dawn, for one thing, as the sun coming up. The last time I'd been in LA, I'd stood at dawn on the balcony of a hotel room on Ocean Boulevard. Beyond the beach some dolphins had come in close to the shore, shattering that glassy surface just beyond the break, the big animals chasing one another around as if joyous about the sunrise, as if drawn to it through the dark water. At that moment it seemed clear that these creatures felt as I did about the dawn. The sun was coming up, rising over the hotel and the city and the San Gabriel Mountains. Dawn that way was good.

Even Galileo had acknowledged the unnaturalness of his modern thought. Those who managed to hold the belief that the earth revolved had actually done "such violence to their own senses," he'd written, "as to prefer what reason tells them to what sensible experience shows them to be the contrary." Maybe he'd said this to mollify his inquisitors, but it made me feel better. With these thoughts and the leap, leap, leap, slap, slap, slap of the water show, I began to relax a little and, as usual when the pressure of insistence is re-

lieved, to think the other. There in the fountain's predict-
able presence, I could by turns appreciate the Cage show,
Cage's alertness, his muscular spontaneity. For Cage, art
was a verb, the action of paying attention. To what was a
secondary matter, if that. This wasn't me—yet, anyway—
but I could understand it. The true path, Cage was suggest-
ing, was the one I was already on, to whatever happened
next. Maybe, I could think by that regulated water, imagining Cage as some big kahuna plying the ocean swell.

The jets rose higher and higher, more of them firing in
unison: The aquafantasia was coming to its climax. When
it did, a group of Japanese businessmen in blue suits posed
for a picture at the critical moment. They lined up quickly
along the catch basin, the front row kneeling as the flood of
the finale roared down from above. Back home they would
look at the picture and recall LA.

The Fossil Watch and Fin-de-Siècle Fizz

The afternoon devolved after that. We shopped. In the MOCA store, I'd looked at the art watches, the Keith Haring Swatch models seeming really old, the eighties and all that East Village stuff already a world away. I owned just one wristwatch, the only one I could not manage to destroy, a thick, black diver's chronometer. Maybe I'd look for another. I mentioned this watch urge to Jess, and she suggested we stop at a place she knew on the way home.

We went for ice cream first, hoping that the sugar would blast us through that four o'clock part of the day. We went into a flower shop where a sleepy and gorgeous woman served ice cream behind a gelato stand. She had to ask each of the four of us to repeat our selections, then dragged her scoop in the barrels.

I sympathized. The ice cream counter had big western-facing windows, and by then the late LA sun was flaring out there, filling the interior with a fusty, floral warmth. I couldn't have concentrated at the ice cream job, either, my hands sticky in the frozen sink, my head in the drowsy heat, and having to remember everybody's flavor as if it were the most important thing in life.

This blue-eyed woman looked as if she'd been up all night the night before. She was a hopeful at the clubs, a singer herself maybe, and a nightly aspirant to stardom; this was her day job, which she was probably praying would be temporary, and probably was.

$\mathcal{D}$own the mall at American Rag, a store of new vintage merchandise, I picked out a wristwatch like Steve's. It was styled like an old watch, its thick numbers in fifties type and almost nerdish, though with a little gold rim. It was called a Fossil, the name supposed to let you have it both ways. Jess helped me choose it and advised me to insist on exactly the combination I wanted. I had to wait as the clerk—an enormous fat man—tried to switch the band with another one I liked better. Those tiny pins eluded him. The others went on ahead, wandering through the mall.

Everything was coming back, it seemed, as if all past moments were regrouping at the end of the millennium, like the characters in a detective story gathering in the study for the climax. We should have been warned, I thought dreamily. We should have known when we made "Woolly Bully" a hit that we would have to hear it for the rest of our lives, albeit in more and more abbreviated versions—behind a jeans ad for a second, or on the radio just long enough for the seek function to pass on to the next station.

Substance didn't even really matter. Deathless ideas, trivia, holy dogma, innocent fashion, castoffs unnoticed at the time, all came back in this effervescent form, the reappearances more and more instantaneous as the moments mounted. This was the time of critical mass, of colliding bits of text, of *fin-de-siècle* fizz.

The fat clerk had to go into the back room and find something to tweeze the pins, and after witnessing this delicate operation and paying a lot for the watch, I found my friends in the next store, collapsed together—clobbered by the ice cream's secondary effect—on a big, soft, down-cushioned, yellow, floral-patterned French Provincial couch that cost $6,000.

Then in slow traffic we headed back, slightly uphill toward the Hollywood sign. Steve said that it had read "Hollywoodland" originally, advertising a real estate subdivision and that the name had spawned Disneyland, where you could go to Frontierland and Tomorrowland. In the thickening traffic, we had to wait a long time whenever we tried to turn left, as the oncoming cars failed and failed to clear. The low western light seemed to be streaming in from far out to sea, slamming into walls all across LA, the city's millions of flat spaces—piers and pavement and patios and rooftops—eventually encroached by shade. For a second I envisioned the original fifty-foot wooden letters of that suffix, stacked in some lot and passing for scrap, their whitewash mostly sun-blasted off: LAND.

Then back at Jess and Steve's, in their study that we had turned into our room, I lay on the futon in the faint smell of housepaint and tuberoses, pushed a pillow behind my head, and went deeply out, hearing as I did my friend Les—who never naps, who has a quasi-religious thing against afternoon napping—still talking with Jess in the kitchen, her words drowning in that hypnagogic roar.

The Fossil ran all right, though a month later the minute hand fell off. One morning the needlelike, phosphorescent green hand was on its own, skittering around like some random indicator beneath the glass. The other hands were pretty useless, I realized, after that. I could approximate the hours on my own. The watch had a little inner dial also, there between the six and the center pin, where a tiny needle clicked around, registering seconds as if each were some separate entity. I never needed this for anything.

I wore the watch for a while, anyway. For one thing, it reminded me of my trip to LA. For another I could refer to it, when late. So I never bothered to get it fixed, this Fossil watch, which from a distance looked enough like an old steady friend from the fifties. It continued to run for a long time, giving me the redundant hours and those instantaneous, anonymous seconds, these and the prospect of its severed minute hand, the only practical one, lying there at the bottom of the dial like some tropical bug's lost leg.

A Man in a Ship May Be Said to Be Quiescent

When I lived in the Midwest I took a rowboat out at night once, onto the windless surface of the lake. The moon stood nearly as round and still in reflection as it seemed in the sky, and the last of the twilight lingered off the stern, shimmering like abalone shell in the stroke, wake, and drip from the oars. During the day, when the surface was choppy, washed by the wind, the mind full of events and company, I could easily assume that I had some discrete existence, solid footing somewhere beneath this constant play of impulse. But rowing at night, moving in solitude into the near-stillness of the lake, those myriad influences down to these few, then for a moment I could know nothing separate, nothing unmoved by everything else.

Newton's concept of absolute time, wrote George Berkeley at the beginning of the eighteenth century, led him to entertain odd ideas about his own existence. The "doctrine lays one under an absolute necessity of thinking either (1) that he passes away innumerable ages without a thought," he wrote, "or else (2) that he is annihilated every moment of his life." Abstracted from the succession of images that marks it in the mind, Berkeley thought, time was nothing.

Newton had posited absolute time, "of itself and from its own nature," flowing "equably without relation to anything external." He'd needed such an absolute as a baseline, and he took the stars too to be fixed, to mark some absolute stillness by which absolute motion might be measured. Said Berkeley, quite before his time, "none of those bodies which seem to be quiescent are truly so." "It doth not appear to me," he said, "that there can be any motion other than *relative*."

Newton's absolute time would not stand, though as a fixed premise it provided a mooring for a few centuries. In this, Berkeley was right. Like Ockham, Berkeley insisted on the uniqueness of specifics. "It seems beneath the dignity of the mind," he wrote, "to affect an exactness in reducing each particular phenomenon to general rules. We should propose to ourselves nobler views."

In terms of "rhythm" in his music, John Cage simply prescribed moments when a player might play, indicating in his notation a range of times for starting and a range for stopping. The piece was performed to a stopwatch, the periods of play (1′30″ to 1′52.5″) made flexible by the player's own decisions to play and to stop within them. So Cage's overall decisions constructed a work out of parts containing the decisions of the players. The music was Zen jazz, chaos in boxes.

Cage said that he wanted the sounds in his music to be free of his intentions, the sounds just sounds, "themselves, that is." "People paying attention to vibratory activity," was all he asked, listeners who listened "not in relation to a fixed ideal performance, but each time attentively to how it happens to be this time."

So the work of Cage's compositions had to be shared— and sometimes even the players didn't want to. In 1964 the New York Philharmonic reacted to Leonard Bernstein's direction of Cage's *Atlas Eclipticalis* with "mob psychology," according to the *Wall Street Journal*'s music critic, Mark Swed. "The orchestra players perceived Cage as a threat to their values," he wrote. Virtuosi after all, they proved capable of "sheer silliness."

A mile down, a motorboat started up, buzzed across the black water, crossed the lake, and shut down. After a while, its wake lifted my rowboat's hull, dripping water from the anchor rope, warping the symmetry of the tree line and stretching the moon. The whole calm dark surface was responding, electric and awake.

Mr. Me at Sundown

I woke up from my nap feeling still gripped by the day and found the pants nested in the cool steel drum of the dryer. I flapped them out and laid them on the top of the machine. The pants were dry and clean, though wrinkled. I could find no tomato juice stains. This was good, as promised in the soap ads. Plus Jessica did have an ironing board. I set it up and plugged the iron in.

The pants had found their wrinkles at random, but now they *needed* to be ironed, was the phrase. So I set to work ironing, standing there in the little sphere of steam, pressing the iron into the cloth, coaxing the fabric flat. As I did, I found myself imagining a friend from back home, a woman devoted to astrology for years, whom I could almost hear arguing that it didn't matter if the constellations didn't actually circle the earth. So what if you were the one going around, even going around backwards? she'd say. In freeze-frame it looked the same. You were still in the same position, relative to the stars. It didn't matter if it wasn't Scorpio rising but you plunging down.

I ironed down one leg and started up the other. It mattered, I thought. Suppose I were taken out under the night sky, blindfolded, spun around and laid on my back, and my blindfold then removed for a second, just long enough for me to get a look at a single star. Would that be a fateful star or just an accidental one? Where was the limit, if your relative position was what counted?

After that I had to concentrate on the unwieldly business of ironing the top of the pants, reinstituting the three creases at the pleats in front, pressing the pocket linings down, working around the zipper and the belt loops. It was actually kind of cute that humanity, rolling through the same starry vista every twelve hours or so, could conceive of night as something palpable. The stars begged for stories, and we had forgotten who'd made them up in the first place, once they'd been venerated into dictates and fortunes.

The finished pants puffed out a little as I held them up, as if legs were already in them. I remembered them dancing in the wash water, as if by their own will. Now they hardly looked like an object at all—they looked like my own intentions in the guise of an object, the way that a car was the intention to go somewhere in the guise of an object. They looked, in other words, the way they were supposed to look.

I didn't know how I felt about that, just then. In part it made me miss the old slow zodiac. I could imagine it punched into sheeted brass, those holes bright from some firelight beyond. The dictates of fortune let you relax. In the presence of fateful stars, you might take it on faith that all these mysterious movements were exactly, if mysteriously, directed. I'd love that kind of fate again, I knew. I folded the pants and put them on top of the dryer.

I went out into the yard where I found Steve, who showed me his garden. The slender black cat named Marlene made her way behind the bushes and around the inner perimeter of the wooden fence as we talked. She was quietly hunting for bugs in the twilight, and I could hear the thump of her pounce in the leaves. High overhead, the last daylight threw into relief wisps of cirrus, invisible all day until now.

Steve pointed out the tall bougainvillea with its spray of violet blooms. They'd thought it was dead, he said, when they'd first moved in. The last tenant had kept it cut way back and had given it no water, and such treatment had kept the plant from ever blossoming. If he could have seen what it could look like, said Steve, he might have tried harder. This plant had just jumped from the ground, given the chance. Under Steve's care, the plant had topped the five-foot fence. It stood above us, blooming like crazy, as if blushing at his praise.

Still, Steve was just a little apologetic about his garden. He'd had to move things around to accommodate the painters, he said, though I couldn't tell what he had moved. The painters had dropped paint chips on the plants, he said, when they prepped the wall above. I noticed these, after he mentioned them. "Those jokers," he said.

Just after he said this, one of the painters went by outside the fence, carrying a ladder. He was finishing up after a long day. I could just see his head and the top of the ladder. His white hat was slopped with all four pastel colors of the four Mission Revival buildings he's been painting. That joker. The cat thumped behind the bushes.

𝒯hinking of time in that redolent yard, I remembered a green bottle that my Uncle Hunter sometime in his youth had wedged into the crotch of a magnolia in that backyard in Pasadena. By the time I saw this bottle, the tree had grown around it, its nubbled bottom protruding from the trunk, and I found it amazing, thinking of the old air, inviolate in there. That was childhood, with its long summer. Now time felt loosened, not just faster but slippery, as if no longer weighted down by the stars. Without the celestial emphasis, time went forward in some completely human way, if "forward" it went.

Where were we? I thought, squinting at the sky. September, it was. Past the equinox already, and summer, too, neither come nor gone, but existing endlessly, as in the movie, a zone in and out of which we rode on the dipping hemisphere. The axle was awry, hence the seasons. And we were a little more than halfway across, tilting back into winter. At the equinox the earth had been plumb in the track of the sun. So this one final, fiery point precipitating out of the afternoon glare should be almost due west. It seemed to be straight out to sea, too, until I recalled the coast faced south a little here. Even in summer at the beach here the sun would seem to wend home northward, toward Malibu— home of the stars, after all.

I went back inside and began to dress for dinner, out of those purple nylon shorts at last. I threw them over the wooden arm of a chair, where they hung like a pelt. Then I put on those smooth white pants, holding off my dislike for them with the thought that at least I was back to square one on that tomato juice suckhole.

That, I was thinking, was that.

In the morning the young monk lay paralyzed, so the abbot sent for help to the Lindisfarne monastery, where some of the brothers knew medicine. When these doctors arrived, they applied "every ounce of skill and knowledge they possessed," writes the Venerable Bede, but to no effect. The youth's paralysis deepened, until, lying there—and luckily enough—he could move only his mouth to speak. He requested some fabric, some bit of Cuthbert's clothing, which had proven incorruptible since the saint's death eleven years before. Some relic was sought, the servant sent to the tomb. He brought back the shoes.

This was about sunset, says Bede. When the abbot put Cuthbert's shoes on the youth's limp feet, the boy ceased suffering and fell into a calm sleep. Hours later the bell for the night office rang, and the youth sat up. After that he stood praying until dawn, thanking God and still wearing those shoes.

Night

The Bush and the Bushel

The way Grant got to LA was odd, though not much odder than the way anyone else got here. Jogging in the dark on Halloween of 1988, on the unfinished interstate leading out of Forney, Texas, Grant was called by the moon. Not that he hadn't been ready to go—he'd been thinking a lot about Los Angeles, anyway. He'd applied to the Art Center in Pasadena as a kind of dare to himself. But until that particular night, he didn't believe he would go. He doesn't really even want to say this, as it's strange, but that night he seemed actually to feel the moon drawing him westward, beyond Dallas, beyond Abilene, all the way to LA.

Grant was twenty-three. He'd been in that small Texas town all his life. His parents had been different from the farmers in Forney and, later, from the Dallas commuters who'd come to live there. His mom and dad had gone to Forney to be landscape painters, to build a house and have a garden and be artists in the country. So Grant had grown up in Forney, under its water tower, on its streets gridded off from the railroad. Out in the flat fields beyond town, the sparse live oaks diminished to the horizon. On a pedestal in front of city hall sat a huge concrete jackrabbit, the town mascot.

Grant went up to Denton for college, and then had gone to Rome for a year, to study art in the ancient heart of the Western world. His girlfriend at the time, Rebecca, had come to visit him, she too wondering what to do next. In the end she'd gone to LA. Grant had gone back to Forney. A year and a half had passed since then. His sense of desperation had grown. Out of this sense of being stuck and of wanting to be ready in case the chance arose, he'd started running. Late at night, he'd put on his running shoes and blast out of the door, sprinting out of town into the dark, as if practicing his exit, getting up to escape velocity.

He was thinking about leaving all the time. In the spring, he'd found out about the Art Center and as a wish had made an application. Then he'd gotten in, a stunner, but there was no way. There was no money. September had arrived, the start of school in LA, with Grant still there in Forney. He'd kept running anyway, fiercer than ever in the night. By Halloween the term was half done.

That night the moon—with no natural illumination of its own—nonetheless shone so brightly that Grant could see the glow reflected on the new yellow lines of the road, the fire of the sun twice cast like a fancy pool shot. Finished and complete, Interstate 20 had its signs already and its overpasses, though it was not yet officially open. Grant had run a couple of miles on the empty road and was muttering, talking to the moon, talking to himself. "Just put your faith in it and do it," he said aloud.

The moon has always seemed to take up the wishes and stories and complaints of human beings on earth, not because it is interested or patient or generous, but because, as a huge mass of inanimate rock and dust, it has no choice. Just then everything was moving—the earth, the moon, Grant—but overall it seemed almost still. Grant made this tiny progress across the prairie and the moon seemed to descend. And even to listen.

He'd run farther than usual already, but his movement still felt effortless, as if his momentum was less than completely his own. Maybe it was the moon, he'd thought, looking at the big yellow globe. Maybe he could feel the moon's gravity, if he tried. He played with the feeling as he ran, turning it off and on as he wanted, and the more he gave into it, the more it felt real, until it shocked him a little with its grip, and for a while he could not disbelieve that his strides simply kept him on his feet, that he flew westward in the pull of the moon, down those yellow lines into the prairie.

Grant leaned in and let it. When the effect waned, he found himself far from town. He turned back, walking now, and sure. It was too late and there was no money, but he was going to LA, never mind that he was still clueless how. He might have dismissed all this, except for an odd coincidence that happened just two days later. Grant's aunt, whom he had not even told about the art school, mailed him some money, and it proved just enough for his tuition. After that, his dad said he could take the cargo van. So after Christmas, on a cold morning, he left. He threw a mattress and some art supplies in the van, said good-bye, and drove out of there, down that same highway, I-20, over the high plains of West Texas, into the deserts beyond, and through a notch in the San Gabriel Mountains. He descended into the LA basin, amazed that he and the city really existed, that he was actually there.

He'd had to sleep on some stranger's back porch in Altadena on that first night, he'd said. The word *stranger* from this blue-eyed, square-jawed kid let me feel that I knew him, the way someone from Forney—where everybody knew everybody—might have known him. It wasn't a word you heard a lot out here.

God foreknew, predestined, called, justified, and glorified Saint Wilfred, who was born in flames. So says Wilfred's hagiographer, a priest named Stephen. The women took Wilfred's pregnant mother to the bed, where she was racked with long pains of labor. Outside the house in the dark, the men waited—as is their lot—until to their shock they saw the house explode. Fire blasted out of the roof into the night sky.

Panic-stricken, the men ran around looking for buckets in the dark. The midwife wiped her hands at the door. "Control yourselves," she cried. "A baby has been born."

Still, the storyteller, the priest named Stephen, knows we are dubious about fire. Fire can be good, he concludes. Recall the blaze beneath the bushel. Remember the burning bush.

The Trampoline

Dusk, evening, nightfall—by the time we left for dinner it was dark, anyway, whatever it was. Day was over. It was time for the universe to recede to stars, to gatherings around separate fires. Just then I could see only one big star through the windshield, a planet probably, Venus perhaps, hanging in the west. On the street, most of the cars had their headlights on, and the traffic blipped by.

Blips—a talk with a friend on the phone, lunch with another once a month—these blips were the story. Taken together they added up to the colorful modern urban whirl, the blip confetti, as we popped in and out. We lived on dozens of channels, each of us channel surfing all the time. That these tiny impulses from others could often feel sufficient —this was the impressive part. It was as if we had the lungs of pearl divers.

What would it have been like, I wondered, never to have left anywhere, never to have come loose like this? Once I spent two weeks with three hundred other people on a mountain in Vermont, and even in that short time became at home with the constant presence of these same people. On the mountain, everyone stayed in the frame. At every meal, the same faces appeared. If you went away, you went only into the middle distance, as it were, maybe to read under a tree.

And so soon we all knew what we all knew. A community could share experience—not *an* experience, like millions of us separately watching an episode of *Seinfeld*—but a single consistent texture of experience that did not stop, that, had we lived on a hilltop in Tuscany in the Middle Ages, would go on not just for our whole lives, but always, and from the first stories. And this was our old home, not the blipping global village but the actual one, a place in which we still lived, if only conceptually.

Steve drove us down Santa Monica Boulevard. In West Hollywood we went by a stylishly bannered traffic island and under lighted billboards featuring gay couples. Then we were out of that part of LA and into whatever the next one was.

When I'd left my little town in Illinois, I'd started on a two-lane blacktop and drove to St. Louis, a route I had taken sometimes before, driving ninety miles to find something like a restaurant. That time, when I'd kept going, I'd launched myself into the cross-country community. On the calm, broad miles of the Missouri interstate near New Flor-

ence, mine had been one car amid a batch that stayed more
or less together for hours. Eventually some of us noticed
one another and waved back and forth, everyone seeming
to share my elation. I liked them all, wished them well. I
passed the caravan of the Mitchell Family Drag Racing
Team, their sleek funny car loaded on a truck and up front
leading the way their splendid van emblazoned with flames
and the family crest. It turned out I would see them, on and
off, for the next two days, in the mountains and on the desert floor.

Near Midway "Turn, Turn, Turn" was on the radio and
mustard blossoms filled the fields for miles. It was Mother's
Day and warm. Some cars seeming to be carrying the moth-
ers, others on their way to seeing them. Other cars looked
desperate, wrecks in flight, with all kinds of stuff tied to the
top. My car was new then—brand-new actually. In my rush
to get out of town, I'd walked into the showroom and said,
"That one." In it, I looked as if I were going on a long vacation, I thought.

It got hot. Sometimes bare feet protruded from a car's
window. At the cutoff for Independence, I caught a glimpse
of two fat girls bouncing like crazy on a backyard trampo-
line. White slabs of limestone had opened in the road cuts.
A mall with a movie went by, among the features *Death-
wish II*. Then Kansas City began to thicken out of the landscape. The Truman Sports Complex bristled from a hillside
among apartment buildings. I found the Royals on the radio, playing just at that moment inside the stadium there.
The place had a crown for a logo, I recalled, and jetting foun-
tains to celebrate home runs.

Kansas began across the river, under the sign of the sun-
flower. In a tollbooth sixty miles from Topeka, two women

jumped up and down, then one of them showed off her engagement ring to the biker waiting to pay. Just after that two great blue herons lumbered over the road, one after the other. April Stevens and Nino Tempo sang "Deep Purple" on the radio—"Breathing my name with a sigh"—then a selection of surf music came on, including "Surfin' USA," from a station in Abilene.

By the third day of my crossing, the enormous west had opened and I could feel that I'd come to that corresponding, freed-yet-firm sense of myself. I looked out at raw rock fifty miles off down a long straight dirt track marked with an arrow and a sign reading, "Point of Rocks." In Nevada there had been towns called Oasis and Deeth and Golconda. The sky over the desert stayed bright a long time into the evening, the rocky horizon sharp in the dry air. I stayed in a motel in Lovelock and the next day crossed the Sierra and descended into Placerville, the San Joaquin Valley like nothing else so far. I still felt happy to be there and sure of myself and my move. I loved California, the whole daredevil experiment of it.

That night in LA we drove to La Farfalle, a Tuscan restaurant. The place had a wood-burning oven and some exposed brick, a high-tech bar with those smoky blue spotlights. They made everybody look good, said Jess, making a face that said that at least they were supposed to. Tracy was there already, holding the table, having made the reservations. She and Jess had been workmates when they had read scripts at a movie studio. I'd met Tracy previously. She was easy to be around. She'd walked over, she said.

Still, dinner was disparate. There was so-and-so and so-and-so, Jess said, pointing to another table. They too were going to Bruce and Tracy's party. Maybe this was their usual place, I thought. Jess went over to say hi.

"Everybody's a little off," she said when she got back, making a quizzical, lips-pursed, eyebrows-raised face.

The waiter came over a couple of times to take our orders, but we put him off, just getting drinks, as Bruce hadn't yet arrived. We just drank wine, not incited much, and talked about the last time we'd seen one another. Jess had gotten us together in San Francisco, and we'd all gone to Square One.

Finally Bruce rushed in, seeming exhilarated. He was starved, he said. He'd been fasting all day.

Taking the Stars to Be Fixed

Not the Empire State Building, not biplanes, not Fay Wray just wanting to get down, but the World Trade Center, helicopters, and Jessica Lange begging the choppers for mercy. Again the big dummy is sticky with fake blood, though in color, which makes it oddly less awful, superconscious red for that slick darkness in black and white. In a ruined silk evening dress and little flats with ankle straps, the girl goes limp, her body enclosed by his big palm. Put down at last on the vertiginous rooftop, she gathers her wits and then, acting in the horrified recognition of what's happening, screams at the helicopters, "Don't kill him! Don't kill him!"

This new version gives the ape more credit. Hearing her scream, he suddenly gets it and looks down at her, an expression of wisdom and compassion sweeping his features.

This is, of course, the moment the gunners have been waiting for. The music howls, and we proceed to the ending, the limp ape mountainous on the street, everyone relieved and returned to normal, except the girl.

Lange said that her work in *King Kong*, her first film role, felt "like it could have belonged to another human being. Obviously," she said in an interview in 1987 published in *American Film*, "it wasn't how I had my career planned out in my mind's eye." She had been waiting tables in Manhattan at the time, at the Lion's Head. "Things shift," she said. "The current changes, and I just decide to go with it."

Carissa was a valley girl. She'd grown up in Encino, graduating from high school in 1981. She doesn't advertise the fact now, and sometimes says she grew up in New York, which is half true, considering that she went to college there. As a child she'd liked to put on shows, and so her mother enrolled her in the summer program at the Lee Strasberg Institute, where they played theater games. One day Lee Strasberg himself visited. He was short and old, Carissa said years afterward, and he had little round glasses "like he did in *Going in Style*." Carissa didn't know who he was then, of course, though that night at the dinner table, her mother made a big deal of it. Imagine! Lee Strasberg had seen her daughter act!

At twenty, she went to NYU and took a degree in theater arts. Mamet spoke to her class, and though his stuff is so male, he said one good thing, one thing she took to heart, which helped her for years afterward. You have to make your own theater, he said. After that she spent a long time developing a one-woman show, a presentation of semiauto-biographical comic sketches called *I Can Fit My Fist in My Mouth*, something she can actually do. Carissa has curly hair, which was blond then. She got Kathy of *The Kathy and Mo Show* to direct her, and premiered the piece in New York in 1989. She won the Backstage Bistro award. Three years later she took the work back home to Los Angeles, where it ran for twelve weeks at Theatre Theatre, and where her mother finally saw it. "That's not me," her mother said.

After that she started looking for Hollywood parts. She got a manager, who got the breakdowns—descriptions of roles sought by Hollywood production companies—and sent her out on auditions. The breakdown description would run something like: "Must be beautiful and be able to roller skate. 18 to 21 years old. Name only." "Name only" meant stars, or at least recognizable actors.

Carissa let her hair go back to brown. Brunettes got more serious roles, like lawyer parts. She began to think more about character, to work on justifying her lines—to imagine being her character and to anticipate what that character might do as a consistent individual. Still, auditions were often a drag. Once she got a callback for a guest-starring TV role, and the guy said, dismissing her, "Next time, don't be so Jewish." A lot of the time, she said, it was about a look and whether your father was in the business.

$\mathcal{S}$he auditioned for a one-line part in *Point of No Return*, the American remake of *La Femme Nikita*, about a training school for female assassins. The breakdown said "Tough," so she went tough, wearing a cap, baggy jeans, and hiking boots. In her scene, the teacher of the female assassins asked her students: "What else can you use as a weapon here?" and Carissa was to answer, in character, "How about this ashtray? You could hit him over the head."

This she did well. She was asked to come back for a second audition later that afternoon with the casting director. That too went well, and she was asked to come back in the morning for an audition for the director. She was given this bit of advice about her tough appearance: "Even more so."

The next morning at home she decided against changing any part of her outfit. It had gotten her that far, and besides, she couldn't imagine anything tougher. She went back to the audition hopeful: After all, it was only a one-line part, and she'd had two auditions already. But she had a shock when she got there. Two other girls had also been called back. They didn't look tough, though. They looked sexy. Tight jeans, bright red lipstick, spike heels. Needless to say, she didn't get the part. She did get the lesson, though, that tough means sexy. "Probably everything means sexy," she said.

Then she got a good break, a part on *Seinfeld*, which was the number one show on TV. She played a salesperson in an antique store who has an affair with George, the insecure short bald guy on the show. George takes her to his house, where he lives with his parents. He lies, saying that he lives alone, and in that context she finds it odd that he has his own baby pictures on the mantle.

Now Carissa is working on her writing. She'd like to write scripts with good parts for women, although she knows that the big audiences—fourteen-year-old boys—are going to see Jean-Claude Van Damme, not Meryl Streep. Even she can't help thinking, as she's writing, "This will be like a movie of the week."

In *Blue Sky*, Jessica Lange plays a military wife, posted to an island in the South Seas with her husband, played by Tommy Lee Jones. He's helping to decontaminate the island from the effects of nuclear testing. The island is idyllic enough anyway, and, in the first scene, Jessica Lange is on the beach, sunbathing in a bikini with no top. Suddenly the sky is full of helicopters. She notices them and stands up, covering her breasts with a silk scarf. The chopper pilots notice her and circle. One of them is her husband, played by Tommy Lee Jones. He smiles familiarly in his tough, military way. He loves that crazy wife of his. We can already tell that she's unusual, for a military wife, and that she could get him into trouble.

She wades out, still waving and pulling off that scarf, exposing her breasts to the tropical sunlight. In the reaction shot, Tommy Lee Jones laughs aloud. He's all right, too, so far. She strides into deeper water, submerging her breasts into the tropical sea. Prop wash batters the surface.

Celestial Instruments

Scene five opens with some monks making fun of the new theory that the earth moves, as Galileo, upstage by himself, looks on. The monks are goofing around, laughing and swaying as they pretend to stand on a rolling globe. They make corny jokes about it. "Don't fall on the peaks of the moon," cries one. As revealed by Galileo's new telescope, even those peaks were heretical, church doctrine claiming the moon to be smooth. Upstage Galileo is not amused. The monks in their black-and-red robes aren't funny; this is the Inquisition, after all. It's also Bertolt Brecht, who knew whereof he spoke—or would, in any case.

Disastrously in Hollywood after the war, Brecht himself oversaw Charles Laughton's performance in the title role of *Galileo*, which Laughton did in his own beard at the Coronet Theater on La Cienega Boulevard. Before the war, when Brecht had written his first draft of the play, he'd made Galileo's abjuration seem foxy, his capitulation to the Church an evasion that allowed him to keep working, to publish his last and greatest book, *Dialogues Concerning Two New Sciences*—as Galileo in fact did.

According to this view, Galileo only seemed to recant, simply paying lip service to the idea of a stationary earth. Good science described the truth anyway, no matter what anyone said. According to one legend, Galileo left the courtroom, walked down the long hallway between the portraits of the cardinals, then at last down the marble steps and out of the Vatican where he stood beneath the Arch of Bells, and, his agreement inside to "abjure, curse and detest my errors" notwithstanding, is said to have stamped on the bare ground and declared, "Still it moves." Never mind the doubt cast on this tale by the record. Actually Galileo, seventy years old and ill, left Rome under guard after this trial, bound for the archbishop's palace in Siena, there to be placed under an indeterminate term of house arrest. Still, the slippery idealist was Brecht's hero in his first draft, before the war.

The redrafted, 1947 LA production sold out its four-week run in advance. Laughton was panicked to be back on stage, so nervous that in rehearsal he kept unconsciously plunging his hands into his front pockets to finger his balls. Opening night was tropical, the audience full of sweating stars, shoulder to shoulder in their seats, Ingrid Bergman, Charlie Chaplin, Olivia de Havilland, Igor Stravinsky among them. On each side of the stage an electric fan wafted the cool trifle from an ice bucket onto the crowd. Laughton found his pockets sewn shut.

According to Otto Friedrich, Brecht found the prevailing fashions in the American theater conventional, despicably so. Primary in his dislike was the convention that the stage should reproduce the illusion of reality. He hated "acting," and he wanted his production to acknowledge its own material life. The actors would not play characters, but be themselves, or at least have a dimension that admitted to their being performers in a play. This was a new idea in 1947, and the Americans in the production—not to mention the audiences in the theater—were still accustomed to surrendering to the illusion, to suspending their disbelief. For them, the concept that the players might have this real dimension was a tough one to grasp.

Of course, things just being themselves might seem like things just being Brecht, under the circumstances. The American company suspected, at any rate, that this broader acknowledgment of theater's reality was only the will of the artist claiming more turf. Difficult Brecht didn't help matters. The rewrite lyricist wanted to clarify the tone of one song, and questioned Brecht. Was the singer praising Galileo? No, said Brecht. Was he criticizing him, then? No, said Brecht, irate in his impatience with these Americans by then.

He feels nothing! he shouted. The singer is standing up there and singing the song because I want him to and for no other reason!

Lulu was back in LA after Greece, where it'd been freezing, she said. She and Bill and a couple from New Zealand they'd met on the train had gotten off in Athens in frigid rain. They were all drunk. Lulu and Bill were continuing the fight they'd begun on the train. They had to walk three miles in the icy drizzle, stumbling under the weight of their backpacks, as they screamed at each other, the New Zealand couple desperate to be rid of them by the end.

"How could you be such an idiot?" she shouted. "Why did I ever agree to go to LA with you in the first place?" And Bill, goaded to it every once in a while, would lash back some terrible remark.

When they reached the hotel, the room was as stark and cold as an icebox. There would be no heat until evening. So they went to bed, just to stay warm, had fierce sex, and slept eighteen hours into the next day.

When they woke up it was snowing. They took the Nikons and went out into it. They climbed to the Acropolis and found it empty. The white stuff whirled among the columns and melted on the warm steps. Lulu went off on her own. She hadn't seen snow since Mount Buller, back home. She wandered around that old place, shooting the snowflakes.

After the war, Brecht makes Galileo recant for real. In the postwar version the astronomer gives in, threatened with torture. "They showed me the instruments," Brecht has him say, by way of explanation. That thought must seek proof in observation, that a thinker must at least attempt to push back preconception, that there is an actual world, one we might reach, that might even unsnare us from history, all this Brecht denies, makes his Galileo deny, after the war.

A month after the production closed, Brecht was served

a summons in Hollywood requiring him to appear in Washington before the House Committee on Un-American Activities. The threadbare server said he didn't mind if he sat down, then complained about his feet, and after serving the subpoena, advised Brecht as to how he might turn a profit on the committee's trip allowance to DC.

Testifying before the committee, Brecht equivocated, quibbled over the English translations of his works, and denied that his writing was based at all on Marx's ideas about history. He denied—"No, no, no, no, no never"—that he had ever made an application to join the Communist Party, and was thanked by the chairman as a good example. Soon afterward, Brecht flew to East Berlin, heading across the Atlantic on Halloween yet, amid the drone of the props.

By then he hated LA, a place, he said, where one could sell a shrug of the shoulders. "In Hell, too, no doubt, these luxuriant gardens, flowers big as trees," he'd written in his journal. "This endless procession of cars."

In those early LA rehearsals of *Galileo*, one long, prophetic, concluding speech had proven too much for Charles Laughton, and Brecht had agreed to cut it. "The universe lost its center overnight," it had read in the translation Laughton himself had penned. "And in the morning it had a countless number of centers. So that now each one can be regarded as a center and none can. There is a lot of room suddenly."

In that cut speech the younger Brecht's Galileo evoked the spheres as a single crystal globe, within which sat the pope and his cardinals, also princes and scholars and merchants and fishwives and children. From this globe, Brecht had written, we are emerging. "Every day something is found."

O early dawn of the beginning, Brecht's Galileo had intoned then. O breath of wind from newfound shores.

Mercy Street

Art school passed quickly. Grant had liked it there and had done well, studying to be a painter like his parents, but when he got out, he was really in LA, and he had no clue as to what to do next. It was a hard time for him. "As much as I knew I was gay," Grant said, "I still didn't want to be." He'd gone out into the desert to check out a monastery, even, and had been surprised when the modern monk there had spoken to him about the collective unconscious. Back home in Venice, Grant decided to make an animation to Peter Gabriel's song "Mercy Street." His favorite line in the song was one about words holding things up, the way bones do.

He worked at home, drawing on a scrim with charcoal, and then clicking his Super 8 camera twice for each picture. He cleaned the scrim after each drawing, using the faint marks of the erasure to compose the next frame. He did twelve drawings for each second of the three-minute song, something more than two thousand drawings in all. The film was autobiographical, he said. In one scene a monk—not like the one he'd met, but a real monk on a pilgrimage in the desert—walked along a ridge top while beyond and above him the sky went to twilight, then night, at last a shooting star arcing overhead.

His friend David was a musician in a band called the Williams Brothers, which had already signed a recording contract. When David saw the animation that Grant had done, he suggested that Grant show it to an executive at the record company. So Grant got an appointment, recorded his little film on VHS tape, and took the freeway over to Burbank.

The record company was a scary place, he said. Everyone was running around, focused on their work in a daunting way. "It was like—what was that movie?" he said. "The one with Kevin Bacon?"

The meeting was a fiasco. He'd arrived with his VHS tape, only to find that down at the record company they all played three-quarter-inch. So he'd had to leave without showing anything. Then it had been expensive to have the piece transferred, though when he did and finally got back in to see the executive, she really liked the animation and wanted more. Would he do a press kit for the Williams Brothers? she asked. She offered him $10,000 to make a fifteen-minute video. Grant could not believe what she was saying. A roll of Super 8 film cost $8.99.

He walked out of there on top of the world, but even before he had arrived back home, he was worried again. From the start he'd wanted to film, not video, though a press kit was usually just videotape of the band talking. He was nervous about shooting in Super 8 and called a friend, who suggested that he use 16 millimeter. Grant had no idea what he was getting into. "If I had known how hard it was going to be," he said later, "I never would have tried." He called a cameraman who said he'd need a Baby Baby and a Shimura 416. Grant had to call somebody else to find out what this meant. All he could do at the time was treat it as an apprenticeship. "This was my break," he said.

With a lot of work, he got the thing shot on 16 millimeter. Then he had to go to postproduction, if for nothing else than to get the film transferred to videotape. He looked in the phone book and found Complete Post, an outfit that sounded right, and took his film over there. He mentioned the record company and the receptionist brightened up and asked if he was the director, and he said he was, though that was the first time he'd really thought of himself that way.

He met with a postproduction representative, both of them under pin spots in a darkened office. Together they mapped out the work they'd do: graphics, telecine, the whole post. Every other word was foreign to Grant—off-line, on-line—but he was impressed. These guys could do morphing. They could make it look like waves. Then the guy under the pin spot added up the bill. It came to $22,000.

After that Grant felt as if he were taking items out of his grocery cart. Just the transfer from film to video ended up costing him most of his $10,000 budget. Complete Post did things like *The Cosby Show*, it turned out. "If I went in there without any name behind me," Grant said, "they would have just gone, 'And?'"

Grant finished postproduction at a dive on Wilshire Boulevard, a place called Video-it, which at $75 per hour was still too expensive. In the next studio a TV evangelist yelled at a lone camera about the New Jerusalem and the end of the world, about locusts appearing as horses armored for battle and wearing golden crowns.

Then when the post was finally done, Grant had to take the tape back to the record company to show the head guy. Grant spent two hours in the outer office, listening to this guy say, "Redo it, redo it" to everyone who got to go in there. At last Grant was called in, and found the guy across a huge, round, shiny table, giving him a look like "Don't waste my time." When they put the tape on, it was the longest fifteen minutes of Grant's life. He only pretended to watch his film, alert to every hint of the head guy's reaction. The head guy leaned back in his chair, stirred around, and seemed not to be paying attention. Then, when it was over, he just said, "I wouldn't change a frame."

Even the guy's receptionist was impressed. Nobody got out of there unscathed, and here was Grant with his little 16-millimeter film, sailing through. So the buzz went around, after that: "Did you see the Williams Brothers press kit?"

About six months later, Grant got a call from the executive who asked if he'd like a real shot. The budget would be $58,000.

Constellation

In Bob Fosse's phantasmagoric musical, *All That Jazz*, Jessica Lange didn't so much play a character, she said, as embody a filmic device. Her vignettes served to further the dilemma of the movie's protagonist. This was frustrating for her, as an actor. The challenge in her art, her joy in acting, was assuming a new character, engaging that personal creation. She loved transforming herself as much as she could, becoming that new entity.

Bruce told me he was good at suspending disbelief in the movies. After he'd seen Jason terrorize the campers, Bruce hadn't slept well. It didn't matter that he'd worked on film sets himself, that he'd participated in the whole jerry-built business that went on outside the frame. When he saw the movie, he let go and believed. By then he was a screenwriter, after all. Of all people, he had to be the one.

Bruce's father made theatrical equipment for Broadway—fog machines and the like—and had helped Bruce get work as a grip on his first film, which was called *Stacking*. Set in the high plains in the fifties, the film was an independent production, and without money for sets, the filmmakers had simply found a one-street town in Montana, a place called Lavina, where the brick-and-wood facades were original, where there were no Touch-Tone phones. Lavina was instant Americana. All they had to do was light it.

Bruce's first task was to drive the grip's white Camaro from LA to Montana. The Camaro had a Hearst shifter, and until he got the hang of it, Bruce was thinking he had to alternate the clutch and the gas, and so stalled it in first at almost every stop. Following the electrician's truck, he drove down the freeway past San Bernardino, then climbed into the desert. The grip had left just three tapes in the car, and once Bruce was out of LA radio range, they were all he played: *The Doors Greatest Hits*, *Blood on the Tracks*, and Bob Seger's *Against the Wind*. Bruce stayed in Las Vegas the first night, then climbed into higher mountains, driving for two full days to reach the location. It was weird, he said, listening to "The End" and seeing all that enormous country.

Lavina lay on the Musselshell River. It was gorgeous, said Bruce. You could see the weather coming a hundred miles away. No matter how good the movie was, it would be like slides of your vacation, compared to that.

Tracy had arrived in LA without intending anything by it, only taking what came. It wasn't some big decision; she had decided to move there as if by a coin toss. When she'd gotten out of Berkeley, she and her roommate, Debbie, had decided that they'd both go back home and find work. Whoever got work first, they agreed, would accommodate the other, until they both had jobs. Tracy's friend in LA found work first.

So Tracy left her parents' home in Danville, a nice enough town in Contra Costa County at the foot of Mount Diablo. Happy to be going, though she might well have stayed, Tracy drove the four hundred miles south to Los Angeles and moved in with Debbie and her parents in Northridge. Eventually the two of them found an apartment in Marina del Rey, which was advertised by its Chamber of Commerce as "real California living." Capping an old estuary, Marina del Rey exists around an inlet that splits the twelve-mile stretch of barrier beach running from the headlands of Pacific Palisades to the cliffs of Palos Verdes. A lot of Marina del Rey is like gold chains and high-rise condos, Tracy said. Some of the apartments have anchorages, boat slips. At Christmas, the Pioneer Skippers put on a boat parade.

She and Debbie found a place just four blocks from the beach, on Driftwood Street, a seventies stucco and wall-to-wall-carpet apartment that always had a little sand in the bathtub. They'd meet guys for margaritas in the evenings, and on Saturday mornings hang out at Coffeeroasters. Sometimes friends from work would drive across the city to meet them at the Cheesecake Factory. The beach was packed with body-building types, with European men in their tiny bathing suits. Jess called them banana hammocks, Tracy said. A few older cottages, bungalows built in the thirties, stood among the beach-front apartment buildings. Tracy would go past them on her walks and want one, a separate house and a real beach place.

Eventually Debbie helped Tracy get a job where she worked, downtown at Banker's Trust in marketing and sales. Not liking the freeways, Tracy took surface streets—mostly Venice Boulevard—inland to work, getting used to the commute and learning what a sig alert was—a one-hour delay. She was a rationalist, Tracy said of herself, a materialist. She didn't have a sense of destiny about her life.

That night at dinner, making conversation and listening to these others, I could hear them mostly taking up where they'd left off with one another in their LA lives. I liked being there among them and just going with that—assuming the texture of the moment—though, when asked about myself, I had to begin at the beginning, which always felt more or less arbitrary, and refer to this and that, explaining myself. So I said what I usually said, blah blah blah, reciting that formula, and recalling Harry, who hated this kind of thing, hated having to come up with a few consistent chronological items about yourself, so that you could appear to intend your identity.

You had to do it, though, he'd said. Otherwise your whole personality might seem like one big suckhole.

Yes, exactly, I was thinking at the table, recalling the short dance that surfers did, that brief, wavering claim at the bottom of a big wave.

*T*racy understood that getting a job "reading" was one sure way of making a living in Hollywood, especially if you were in the union. Through a friend she heard about an opening at a major studio, and by chance the guy who was interviewing for an assistant had been in commodities trading before, and so her bank job turned out to be a perfect stepping stone. He didn't care that she had no experience in the entertainment business. For him it was a plus.

They worked for the live-action, maybe-for-kids division of the studio, a fledgling operation then. Their first film starred Jeff Daniels. In it spiders threatened to take over the world. After that they did one about a kid who gets in trouble with the mob and has to run, run, run. Then they made the bad baby-sitter movie and the one about the adventurous doctor seeking a cure for cancer among the tribes of the rain forest. Eventually, they'd do the corrupt TV show film and the one about the caveman in the San Fernando Valley.

Tracy liked working on the classy old studio lot, which was a gated village, self-contained like a college campus. People rode around in golf carts, and there were bike messengers and a commissary where everybody ate together, actors and set builders and executives. Tracy got her dry cleaning done there, also her car repairs and haircuts. In the

forties on the lot you could bunk there, not going home
even to sleep until a picture was done.

She worked in a cubicle among cubicles, with the bosses'
offices on the periphery. One day a young screenwriter
came in for a meeting with the producer in the office next to
Tracy's boss. As he stood around waiting, he said hi. That
was Bruce.

Once Tracy got into the union, she started writing coverage right away. Writing coverage was the work of sifting
through scripts. It was like panning for gold, she said. She
had to do a formulaic synopsis and comment for each script.
She'd read maybe four hundred scripts a year in the four
years since she'd gotten onto it full-time. At the bank she'd
had to wear pantyhose every day. Writing coverage she
could work at home and wear anything she liked.

The scripts came from agents representing writers, and
about twenty percent of them were OK, she said. Sometimes she'd get a script that was directed at a particular director or star. Sometimes these scripts came with these
people already attached. Those were hot scripts.

Of course there were tons of lousy stuff. Action scripts
had lots of directions for fighting and just bits of dialogue
like "Puny harmless maggots!" This was an actual line from
a Viking script she'd read. She and the other readers also had
a term for unwarranted dialogue indications, set in paren-
theses between the character's name and what was said.
They called them "wrylies," as in HILDEGAARD (wryly):
"Puny harmless maggots!"

When Bruce slept, up there in Montana, he slept on the floor of the wardrobe room. Night exteriors were the worst. Then you were up all day and all night. Just darkness at night wouldn't do, he learned. Ordinary night would look like a black hole on the screen. You had to light a few things—a facade above the block, a steeple, a storefront—to show that it was night, by comparison.

Twice they had to light the whole town. In the heat of the day he worked as they wired the facades, hauling coils of four-aught cable, fifty feet at a pound per foot. Then he helped hang the lights, as someone on the street below called out if the cabling was going to appear in the shot. It was work. Bruce was outside all the time. He was up all night and hungry a lot. He had to change a $2,500 twelve-hundred-watt bulb at the top of a ladder in the frigid wind while somebody yelled at him. Then there were the actors. He couldn't believe the actors. Frederic Forrest, Christine Lahti, Megan Fallows. Up there, in Lavina, they had to look good. They had to be perfect. They had to take direction for eighteen hours straight.

On the set of *Tootsie*, Jessica Lange was surprised to see how her approach as an actor differed from Dustin Hoffman's. For one take, the script required Hoffman to come into the camera's frame, say just one line, and then exit. Lange said that she would have come prepared and simply said the line—end of take. Hoffman did his single line dozens of times, each time saying, "Keep the camera running, just keep it going."

"He ran in and said the line and he ran out and then ran back in," said Lange. Among all those takes was the one that would finally appear in the film.

Red MoM's

Urban, the pope who condemned Galileo, paid a monthly fee to an occult consultant, one Tommaso Campanella, a Dominican friar and an expert in magic and astronomy. Brother Tommaso had written on fate and the stars and had penned as well a popular utopian volume, predicting the defeat of the heresies and the institution of world rule by the Church. This City of the Sun (so his book was called) would be ruled by a pontiff not-so-coincidentally resembling Tommaso's benefactor, Urban.

The pope identified himself with the sun and feared eclipses. The complete darkening of the sun might cause his own death, which he likewise feared, of course. So, learning that an eclipse would occur on June 10, 1630, he sought Brother Tommaso's advice. Wear white robes, said Tommaso, and shut yourself in a darkened room.

In this room the pope and his counselor burned myrtle and laurel and drank spirits distilled in specific months to counter the influences of Saturn and Mars. The astrologer then arranged a model universe of crystals and candles, with this toy intending to steer the stars.

And apparently succeeding. For on June 10, the path of total darkness passed to the north. Sufficient corona shone and the pope was spared. Tommaso may have been lucky or may have simply studied the charts, but in any case Urban survived, able to go on waking up each morning after that, and seeing first thing at the foot of his bed—no matter what the actual weather—a golden mural of the rising sun.

Tracy and Bruce lived in an upper flat in a Moorish-looking apartment building, a stucco creation from the twenties that stood behind a row of sycamores on Sycamore Street. It had a terra-cotta roof, steps surmounted by a Spanish coat of arms, and above that a delicate, turreted balcony, just big enough for one person. That Spanish balcony with its wrought-iron railing was a note to centuries of architecture, to a style that had come across the Atlantic with the conquistadors, to be recreated in America for nostalgia's sake, finally reinvented for the Mission Revival LA of the Bogart Period. Though the balcony was now just one bit, one item in the pastiche, I couldn't help feeling enamored, Hollywoodish.

Back in San Francisco, I had spoken on the phone with a friend who has worked in and around Hollywood for years. This would be my first Hollywood party, I'd told him. Real Hollywood people don't go to the parties, he'd said. Only new people went to them. If he had to go to a party for some reason, he couldn't wait to get out of there. None of this deterred me a bit of course. According to his formula, I was perfect. Having arrived that morning, I could hardly have been newer in town.

And just then the balcony looked to me like a setting for a classic star, for someone like Lauren Bacall, whom I could imagine up there, in an evening gown and waving languidly, her pale arm gloved above the elbow. Maybe she would glance into the depths of the balcony, say something ironic and charming to someone who'd rather not be seen, then turn elegantly, delightedly back.

Being entirely actual didn't seem quite possible—or even desirable—in such a setting. Such a fantasy was what Hollywood had always been about. Years before in LA I had stayed in the Hollywood Hills in a house designed by a Disney animator as a small Bavarian castle. The wow of it got oppressive after a while. But this balcony was just a touch, after all, and I let myself fall for it, or at least for Lauren Bacall.

We were buzzed in and started up a broad staircase. From the landing I could see the inside of the balcony, which wasn't anything. A high window bearing a stained-glass rose sealed the opening. At the door our dinner companions and now our hosts ushered us in. Their apartment was big and clean and bright, sconces illuminating every wall. The living room had a ceiling fan and fancy plasterwork around the fireplace, a jar of candy corn on the mantel. The wooden floors looked blond and new, and the place seemed to go back for blocks. In the dining room, a necklace of interlinked gold letters—HAPPY BIRTHDAY—had been strung across the mirror, and a bunch of balloons bobbed against the ceiling. They'd put out chips and salsa and guacamole and spinach dip in a hollowed-out loaf of bread.

The balloons scared the cats, said Tracy. They had three cats, she added, gesturing down the long hallway to the darkened bedroom where the bravest one, a gray-striped creature with a white apron and paws, peered out toward our human realm with alarm.

After the preliminaries I let the others talk and hung around the front windows, appearing to look out and actually feeling a little shy. It's always a strain, meeting stranger-to-stranger like that, and down there in LA, where I was out of it, it seemed more so. The sycamores, crisp and autumnal and seeming eastern, stood a few feet outside, their leaves lit by the interior lights of the room. I looked at them, stalling and indulging only long enough in my habitual speculation to consider what a big step steady illumination had been for human beings, a leap into a world of our own, bright when we wanted and dark when we said so.

It turned out I needn't have worried about meeting anyone. Everyone was fine. The party proved regular enough. It had the regular party items, chips and onion dip and a punch bowl. Its regularity, its warm Everytown USA quality seemed solid and real, as if wood grained. Afterward I remembered my friend saying that the real Hollywood people wouldn't be there, though the ones who were seemed actual enough.

Guests arrived in bunches and got drinks. The noise rose. I finished procrastinating by the window, then ventured into the crowd, heading ostensibly for the food. At the punch bowl I met a guy named Grant, a director of music videos it turned out. I drank the spiked punch and picked red M&M's out of the dish, as we tried to introduce ourselves.

Vaquero in Chaps and Bandanna

In Brooklyn early in the century, Lloyd's grandfather had been a cutter in the garment trades, his specialty being ladies' coats and dresses. He cut the female form into piles of fabric, using a sharp, hooked knife. Even as an old man, Louis, married to Lloyd's maternal grandmother, Bess, had a great grip from working with that knife. Also a scar from one bad accident, a lifelong mark that fascinated his grandson.

A speculator, a gambler and not a successful one, Louis smote himself with loss playing poker, Lloyd said, and when he'd lose, he'd take off. The first time he'd abandoned his young family and had gone out to San Francisco, where he'd finally had to fall back on his skill as a garment cutter. His new boss, a moral man, had insisted that Louis bring his family out from back East and so he sent train tickets for Bess and the three kids.

If the boss had intended to ensure steady work from Louis, the ploy didn't succeed, as Louis continued to gamble, in time hocking the furniture and disappearing again. Bess went to work slinging hash in downtown San Francisco as the Depression began. Her daughter, Florence, dreamed of becoming a ballerina and actually danced with an enormous silver balloon in a presentation for the Garment Workers' Union, though afterward her returned-for-the-moment father forbade her from doing further theatrical work—it wasn't proper for a young woman.

Florence attended the High School of Business and Commerce and hoped in those dire days to marry a rich man. She met her future husband Henry in the neighborhood at age fourteen, but she didn't choose him at first. At seventeen, working at Weinstein's Department Store, she met a Gentile boy, and when their romance didn't work out, went back to New York, taking the train for a prolonged visit to her cousins. There, in the depths of the Depression, she didn't happen to meet anyone else, only young guys looking for rich girls.

Back in San Francisco, Henry the future husband was putting his career together, going to the California College of Chiropody and coming out a hand and foot specialist, a chiropodist. When Florence returned from the East, he pursued her again. Eventually they married. She went back to work in the accounting department at Weinstein's Department Store, then took a job at US Rubber, where she had to hide her Jewishness and, later and as long as she could, her pregnancy. She was twenty-four in 1937, when she gave birth to Lloyd.

Lloyd's father the chiropodist set up his office over Zinke's Shoe Repair, a practical if pedestrian arrangement. Zinke, looking at the patterns of wear on the shoes that came in, could refer his customers upstairs to Henry. Henry, looking at his customers' feet, could likewise refer them to the shoe specialist below. Henry's father had driven a horse-drawn truck for San Francisco's Langendorf Bakery; his father's father had been a Polish dairy farmer, living near the village of Stuchin. Before that, the history of Lloyd's male ancestors, the line called Amrofel—the name "of Raphael" in Hebrew, changed to Hamrol on Ellis Island—is obscure. Perhaps they were among the people who went north at the end of the Middle Ages, when Ferdinand and Isabella (those same monarchs in that same year, 1492) expelled the Jews from Spain where they'd lived for more than a millennium, since Jerusalem's destruction by Rome.

Growing up in postwar LA, Lloyd became an artist. In the 1990s he built his studio in a warehouse just east of downtown, in an area of light industry near the Vernon district, where he and the other tenants of the warehouse constructed a kind of artistic enclave, even importing trees in tubs to shade the narrow street out front. There they lean on the fenders of their pick-ups in the cool of the morning, sip coffee, and stretch out their talk, extending a little the moment before work.

In the studio, Lloyd says things into the phone receiver like "The face rock is from Red Mountain Mining," or "A light to medium sandblast." The studio itself is jammed. Stuff loads the counters: tools and artwork and lumber and stone, amid that clutter a fist-sized chunk of black volcanic glass, a set of small square bottles of enamel paint—Testors—a cardboard model of Lloyd's new stone sculpture for

Caltech, a spiral, its slightly graduated section rising a little taller than the head of the tiny figure of a human being glued down next to it.

One seven-foot shelf bears dozens of boxes of nails in various sizes, each bearing the bold, redundant label, NAILS. On the floor an ancient, blackened wooden crate—"Seven-Up Bottling Company of Los Angeles"—holds coils of copper wire in various gauges. Another box, packed with one-inch cubes in primary colors—"Developmental Learning Materials"—sits on a shelf beneath a wall bearing a set of Lloyd's pieces that look like bright, oversized, interwoven popsicle sticks. Furniture and tools fill the floor space: a band sander and a drill press, workbenches, light tables with loupes, steel cabinets, a fridge, and a TV with an old stuffed chair in front of it, where Lloyd's dog Shantah likes to sleep when she isn't sleeping on the couch by the door.

It's a place of particular, often mysterious objects. Visiting there one day I picked up a cardboard tube, its yellowed label depicting a cooked turkey and reading "© 1946." Inside was a baster, a delicate object made more so by age, its tube of tapering glass and its rubber squeeze ball by then hard as a wooden knob. It had come from Louise's mother's house, Lloyd said, and hadn't been used for years. Though it was of no further use for basting, he liked it. His own mother had one like it when he was young. He'd held onto this baster, bringing it to his studio without fully knowing why. This was his prerogative as an artist and actually the source and soul of art, this ability to allow an impulse to exist and manifest itself in objects without requiring of them a conscious reason or an excuse, only responding to a personal feeling of rightness, of connection—pure particularity, insisted upon, observed, apprehended.

At three, Lloyd had been a cute kid who got colds a lot and didn't gain weight on schedule. When he'd showed some lung weakness, the doctor's recommendation that Lloyd get out of San Francisco's wet climate had coincided with Henry's dissatisfaction with his job—he was by then working for another chiropodist. Lloyd's father had gotten the LA newspapers and within a couple of weeks the family was on the road south, driving down 99 through Modesto in their 1931 Ford four-door, a green-and-black sedan with yellow wheel trim. It had no fuel pump, said Lloyd fifty years later in his studio, just a gravity feed for the gas, right in front of the windshield.

Henry and Florence left their extended families in San Francisco and moved to LA, never to return. Eventually they'd rented an apartment in a Spanish stucco fourplex on Sierra Bonita near Beverly. Henry had opened a chiropody office in the Famous Department Store downtown, and Florence had worked at Pep Boys, doing running inventory. As the war years proceeded, Lloyd had drawn battle scenes at school. He'd played with his friends on the roof of the apartment buildings. They'd liked especially the illicit pleasure of restoking the incinerator fire in the burner up there. On Saturday mornings he'd gone to the serials at the Pan Pacific Theater, watching good guys in capes chase swarthy alien saboteurs. He'd seen John Payne in *Back to Bataan* and later, as a young teen at the Loyola, had fallen in love with Yvonne de Carlo in her role as a harem dancer.

By then his father had found a new house in Westchester, in a subdivision adjacent to LAX now vanished into airport parking lot C. It had seemed rural and a little isolated out there by the airport, in a single-family house. In the open country, Lloyd and his friends dug trenches for hideouts in the neighboring fields.

The beach was close. Lloyd and his Westchester High buddies would go to Del Rey Beach and build a bonfire in one of the fire pits there, hoping to end up under a blanket with a girl. By then the die was pretty much cast, or at least it would be when Lloyd as a youth of sixteen was selected for the special class at the Chouinard Art Institute. There he saw the naked model and fled the classroom, overpowered and sure that he, not the model, had been the subject of the class's attention. Still, this episode made its profound impression. His parents at that point had been gently directing him toward medicine or something similar. Dentists had hours from ten to two, he was told. But by then Lloyd had his own ideas. So he sums up the events of his early life, only half in jest: the move to LA, the birth of his sister, the dropping of the atomic bomb, the naked model.

Plus there was Jerome "Chick" de Rollin, Lloyd's art teacher at Santa Monica College, who with his beret, mustache, and string tie had a studio in a castle and horse farm in Carbon Canyon, and whose art history lessons stopped before cubism, after which modern art had become an intellectualized disgrace. Chick painted and rode and smoked; he had soirées with classical music; he wore only a loincloth some days, it was said. Lloyd was wowed, by then, and ready to be off on his adventure in art.

For his first public project, Lloyd assisted in the making of a mural illustrating the arrival of Spaniards in the Los Angeles Basin. The mural depicted in continuous narrative Cabrillo's galleons arriving in 1542—the year before Copernicus published his celestial theory—then the conquistadors in their hauberks, the priests in their medieval robes, the vaqueros in their chaps and bandannas. Lloyd prepared the tinted lime plaster for the fresco and modeled for the artist, who put Lloyd's face in the work, painting it onto a cowboy on horseback. Viewed from Santa Monica Bay, the wild, fertile basin appeared partially obscured in haze, the plumes of smoke from native fires flattening at a distinct level above the plain and the body of water in the foreground labeled, as the Spaniards called it, "Bahía de los Fumos."

Lloyd and Louise hike almost every morning in Griffith Park, climbing the hills there above the city with their dog, Shantah, who knows the way. Occasionally the dog will take off into the chaparral after a rabbit or a squirrel or a coyote or something else that Lloyd never sees. The hills are covered with scrub oak and laurel and jimsonweed above, sycamores in the wetter canyons below, and down there also the occasional, imported, artificially watered redwood—a ridiculous thing, according to Lloyd.

In the park, the three of them usually take the closed roads that wind from Hollywood over the ridge to the Valley. Sometimes they climb the continuation of Vermont Avenue past the Greek Theater. The road forks below the Observatory and goes through a tunnel with a perfect vault—built before plywood, says Lloyd, so that the cement bears the grain of the individual boards that composed the mold. When they emerge from the tunnel, they look out westward across the city toward the sea, above the smog blanket. "High up in the park," Louise wrote in one of her delicious, literary letters. "Bliss."

From the top of the park, Louise and Lloyd have seen LA in fog, in bright clear winter air after rain, and on those awful days, the heat blasting already at 7 A.M. "I hate those days," says Lloyd, narrowing his eyes. They even witnessed a solar eclipse once from those heights, and once came upon four men attaching spiraling tubes and wires and gauges and other gadgets to a large wooden box. Louise asked if it was an Orgone box, but they'd never heard of that. Then Lloyd figured it out. "Aliens," he said.

"That's right, aliens," said one of the movie crew carpenters. "They keep us all working."

Perced to the Roote

So anyway I felt a little out of it at the party. My own career to date in Hollywood had consisted of a rather-too-short series of phone calls. A studio actor had read a book of mine, and had asked his production person to call me to say that he'd liked it. Though it was odd to know how to respond to such reportage, I appreciated the call, which I took as purely complimentary, not as business interest.

A film of that book had never seemed possible. I could imagine it as a movie in only two ways: either as some kind of procedural narrative—like a shop manual—studded with odd objects, or as a large-screen epic with lots of action and a cast of thousands, but without any close-ups, all of which would have been of me. Neither seemed like any movie I'd seen lately.

Still, this movie actor—a star yet—had liked the book.

Like most people, he had a personal reason. Much of the story was set on the Oakland docks, where he'd spent time as a child, working on a boat with his father. If I was ever in LA, said his production person, he'd be glad to meet me. Naturally I assumed he meant the star. It just so happened, I said, that I *was* coming to LA, oddly enough.

We set a tentative date. It made me nervous to think of meeting someone I'd only known from his movie personae. Would he be dull in person, as if deflated to life size? Or would he act like one of his characters? I'd heard of actors from the soaps answering to their characters' names in public for the sake of their confused and adoring fans. Or maybe this guy would have a special role worked out, a character he assumed for purely complimentary, nonbusiness meetings. If so, how could I, an amateur actor at best, ever compete?

Then there were my odd associations with his roles. I'd seen this guy in various movies, some serious, even distinguished, but I couldn't stop recalling one movie in particular as the date for our meeting approached. In this comedy the actor, dressed only in his underwear, had wrestled with a big dog. Now actors such as De Niro put themselves through grueling physical trials to approximate the characters they have to play, but the more I thought about the actual business, the more I was impressed by the sheer nerve it would take to strip to your underwear and wrestle a dog, as grown men and women stood around with clipboards and took film. I had to hand it to him, really. Still, I knew that at our meeting I wouldn't be able to stop thinking about that dog scene.

But I needn't have worried about meeting this actor, it turned out. A couple of days before the meeting, his production person called to say that he regretted that the star regretted that he would have to put off the meeting. After that we spoke on a few occasions, but could never quite find an available date, though finally he said April would be good. Yes, he said, definitely, tentatively in April.

Penelope Spheeris's *The Beverly Hillbillies* enlarged on the popular television show created by Paul Henning in the early sixties. The movie repeated the concept and even some of the situations of the TV show. As in the old TV show, Jethro rents a billboard to advertise for a wife. Granny drives a motorcycle into the swimming pool. Despite these similarities, though, the film's overall effect was quite different.

The TV show was a burlesque of the prophet leading his people to the promised land, oddly harking back to that American Exodus, *The Grapes of Wrath*. It evoked, ironically, scenes of flight to California during the Dust Bowl, of Okies set adrift in the thirties, all kinds of stuff tied to the tops of their old trucks. By the rich sixties the depression seemed safely behind us, and these scenes became available for camp. The Joads became the Clampetts, hicks arriving in Tinseltown, even Granny tied to the top of the truck.

In Spheeris's 1994 remake, everything is bigger, faster, and louder. For one thing, the Clampetts can't be mere millionaires. We know that a million won't buy that house. Also when Uncle Jed accidentally struck oil in the TV show, black fluid seeped from the ground. In the movie, the explosion of his shotgun blast triggers three fifty-foot gushers, and Jed's strike proves larger than the oil fields of Kuwait. Now that's bubblin' crude. Behind the opening credits and familiar song, the black torrent drenches Jim Varney, star of *Ernest Goes to Camp*, who replaces Buddy Ebsen in the lead. The new film rocks along, careering to a soundtrack studded with country classics—"Hot Rod Lincoln," "Crying Time." The shots move at an MTV pace, in fast bits to music. Plus LA has gotten a mite anxious since the days of Camelot. When the Clampetts arrive at their mansion and are mistaken for armed burglars, an LAPD SWAT team roars in, padded and bristling with armaments.

In the Bible, Jethro was the father-in-law of Moses; in *The Beverly Hillbillies* he is Jed's idiot nephew. Played on TV by Max Baer, Jr., son of the heavyweight champ, the role in the remake fell to a tall, dark actor who bore some resemblance to the earlier Jethro, and hence, coincidentally, to the champion boxer as well. In one scene from the movie, Jethro drives the Clampett truck too slowly on the freeway, irritating another driver, who flips him off. "I reckon that's the way they wave howdy out here," says Jethro, whose specialty is mistaken signs. Such ignorance is the main vehicle for humor in the film, as it was in the original show, which was overall a series of ironic jokes about good-hearted country people simply not getting it, though they prove wiser, finally, than the city people who do.

It was the "Most Fun Film in Decades!" wrote Barry ZeVan in *Channel America*. But not a box office bonanza, like Spheeris's *Wayne's World*. The theory must have been that the show's popularity in the sixties would translate to the nineties and make *The Beverly Hillbillies* a megahit. If anyone might have pulled this off, it was Spheeris. Her light touch with such thick material had been evident since her Decline and Fall documentaries, particularly the winning *Part II: The Metal Years*.

But alas, the zeitgeist. The TV success of *The Beverly Hillbillies* depended on the audience's consisting in large measure of people who feared they might be rubes. Hence the joy in the show's irony. But now hillbillies have satellite dishes and watch the Bravo channel or at least *The Lifestyles of the Rich and Famous*. Now they get it. No rubes they.

All we have to do is pump it up, somebody must have proposed. We're still as slow and innocent as we were back then, just faster and more experienced.

In some of the stories I heard at the party, Hollywood posed its tantalizing promise, the torment of development hell. I spoke to one writer who had succeeded in having his work optioned, who spoke wistfully of his stories someday appearing on the screen. That light glimmered out there, maybe a mirage. Then an actor spoke to me of trying out for weird roles, of proceeding away from herself to express her real essence. I was beginning to think that maybe the promise of the town withdrew at one's approach, no matter how well one did here. Definitely, tentatively in April, I recalled.

Then one guy arrived, entering the party late amid a crowd of admiring friends. He was a beautiful man, tall and young and happy, having been just that day on the set of his first star-credited film. He'd been acting the part of Jethro in a remake of *The Beverly Hillbillies*, and he seemed to be surfing, gliding through the party on the sheer promise of it.

Hills, that is. Swimming pools, movie stars.

People Who Say Yes

The lights went off and the glowing cakes came in, one chocolate and one white with berries, both from Sweet Lady Jane's. We sang, the groan of that old tune rising as usual to a shout at the end, as Jess's friends pitched in. "Happy Birthday" is a silly song, but seemed then perfectly effective, gladdening everyone, not only Jess, and rendering the occasion happy. Jess beamed as she leaned over the candles, then disappeared into the dark when she blew them out. The lights came back on amid hooting and applause.

Later we gathered around Jess in the living room. She sat on the couch at the center of the group, opening her presents. Here's what she got: a candelabra-topped picture frame, Barbara Kingsolver's *Animal Dreams*, a pair of earrings shaped like tiny black metal chairs, raspberry coffee, a blank bound book, a silver pen and holder, a perfume bottle with one of those sleek dippers, and an old, thick, leather-bound volume, its title gold-leafed on the spine, its endpapers marbled, its text an appreciation of Shakespeare. These items Jess examined and praised, thanking the givers and holding up each gift in its turn.

Few people in town, I was told, could really say yes, maybe a dozen at the outside. And if you worked as an assistant for one of them, you had to be flexible. You did everything. An assistant to someone who could say yes might read scripts, go to test screenings, offer his opinion, schedule the studio jet, and, if the wife found authentic tiles in Provence that resembled the copies on the terrace back in Bel Air, might deal with their insurance and shipping and finally drive out to the villa to videotape their arrival.

They'd bought the neighboring estate, intending to tear it down, to give the property a rolling and unbounded prospect. In the process they had decided to have their own place redone. The assistant was to shoot the work—the reconstruction of the terrace, the addition of a balcony to the master bedroom, the construction of a wing for the servants—then send the tape back to the Côte d'Azur, so they might see how their work was proceeding.

He taped the foremen, who looked like sunny muscled surfers, and the Hispanic workers, who joshed him about his attempts to speak with them in *español*. He shot all of them as they stood around with their arms crossed as the crates from France came off the truck, then as they set about opening the crates, and inspecting each of the gorgeous tiles, which were old terra-cotta, their surfaces awash with umbers. He took selected shots of the crew hand-cleaning the tiles after that, work that took a week.

There was just one problem with the tiles, which turned out to be major. The new tiles, which were actually centuries older, proved slightly smaller, and this small difference, magnified across their collective area, changed the dimensions of the entire terrace, which changed everything. She'd bought all the tiles, of course, so there was no question of getting more from Europe to make the area the same. So the architect had to be called, the landscaping redone. The assistant had to buy more tape.

$\mathcal{T}$he studio jet flew higher than commercial aircraft, up through the thin air of the stratosphere, where there was no turbulence, so the ride was smooth. Inside, the Gulfstream was lavish, a flying living room from which you might emerge on the other side of the world quite refreshed, as if the Côte d'Azur had come to you while you were hosting a little fête in your vibrating lounge.

Except when they took the Concorde to save time, the people who could say yes always flew in the jet. No one else at the studio did, though. This jet was a winged bonus. People who had special relationships—stars, mostly—got to use the jet, as a come-on or a contract sweetener or a big thank-you. If a star wanted to book the jet, to go to Cannes or bring artwork or a nanny over from London or Prague, his or her person called the hangar attendants at Burbank. The attendants always replied that the schedule looked full and then called the assistant, who would ask.

Or if the personage of potential yes wanted, hypothetically, to give B. B. King's guitar, Lucille, as a birthday present to a person with a special relationship to the studio, the assistant might have to call B. B. King and try to talk him out of his guitar. If he succeeded, he would arrange payment, always surprised, when the sky was the limit, to see how low the sky was. Then, when the gift arrived on the lot, he might order one of the craftspeople on the medieval village that was the lot to construct and engrave a plaque clarifying what this instrument with its shapely *f*-holes signified—which otherwise might have seemed like just some other red Gibson—and naming the parties, B. B. King, if that's who it was, as well as the yes person, and the person with the special relationship, and, of course, Lucille the guitar.

Sometimes somebody else's people would send gifts to his person's people, and so he would just get these things, weird, well-packaged, expensive, meaningless presents: Swiss chocolates, books of photographs by Herb Ritts, Wild West antiques. You could punt them into the sea and feel nothing.

It was always ambiguous. Sometimes they might almost have seemed to be friends. Sometimes the person who said yes asked him for a ride to work, and they would pull up to the gate in his little Jetta, making the guard jump. At times like these, they might speak cordially, informally, the deference everyone showed him a little muted, the subject the LA Kings or whatever.

Usually, though, the assistant drove to work alone. Like a lot of people in LA, he was secretly fond of this solitary commute. He had no car phone, and in the slow traffic, he'd turn up the air-conditioning and feel insulated behind his shades, deliciously impossible to reach, disconnected from all of it for the moment and safe. He'd crank the tape player and sing, sealed in among other cars containing other drivers, some of them singing as well. A tide had flooded in, it felt like, covering the connections and leaving him on his own tiny, sunny island.

In the end he'd decided just to shoot the tiles straight. He'd simply document them, their arrival, their installation, and the rest of the unbelievably elaborate work, just taking videotape, thank you very much. He didn't try to be artistic, though the thought had occurred to him, that if he'd wanted to be a director, here was the chance. Maybe he could shoot the work on the house in some avant-garde way that would delight them, even get watched again just for fun, over there in the South of France. But these were images of construction processes, step-by-step adhesion and grouting and the like, which you couldn't even edit, really, because they had to be in the order they were done.

Beyond that, the bulldozers and crane—before this job he'd never imagined individuals actually rented stuff like this—the flags and string and cut lawn, the raw beams and pouring cement, splayed wiring, scattered Californian dirt, with only the workers to enliven the frame, all this left him with just the possibilities for a voice-over, which weren't enough.

A man went to live as a monk, on the Island of Delights in the far western sea. After a year, his father sailed over to visit him. Many monks lived on that island. Their cells honeycombed the cliffs, and when his father's boat drew up to the dock, they swarmed out and climbed down in their brown robes to greet him.

The son rejoiced greatly to see his father, and that evening after Compline the two walked together in the dark, talking and making their way down to the western shore, where they happened to find a small boat moored. The son proposed that they row out onto the calm sea.

Fog engulfed them on the water, and they pulled nowhere, each on an oar for an hour or two, even the stern of their little boat lost in thick mist. At last a light appeared ahead, emanating from a broad green shore. They landed, and under a seemingly bright sky ventured inland, through fields of flowers and forests of fruiting trees. In this way they walked for what seemed an enchanted fortnight, even the stones beneath their feet luminous, gems.

Then they came to a river. On the far shore stood a radiant individual, who called to them, warning them that as mortals they might go no farther, but bidding them nonetheless be of good cheer. "The Lord has shown you this land," he said, "intended for his saints."

Still, they could not cross the river. "Go back therefore," said the radiant one, "the way you came."

"Who are you?" called the father.

"For a year," said the radiance, "you've walked in daylight, needing no sleep; knowing neither thirst nor hunger. Why then do you not rather ask about this place?"

The father and son returned to their boat and rowed back through the same thick fog, finding their old shore. Their brethren, relieved to see them, rebuked them anyway for abandoning their sheep for so long, and on the bluff, even.

"Smell our garments, brothers," said the son. "We have been to paradise."

Pioneertown

Grant drove home to Venice after the meeting. The record company executive had asked him if he'd known what a treatment was and he'd said he thought so, and now was going home to write one, whatever one was, to come up with some images for the song by the Greenberry Woods and to figure out what in the world he was going to do with $58,000.

The song, which she'd played him just once on a tape that sounded third-generation, was set in Paris, where the singer bid a French girl good-bye. "Adieu," it was called. "I knew a change was going to come," was the opening line of the bridge. In the record company office, Grant had to gather together the presence of mind to listen to the song.

"Dream about it," she'd told him as he'd left. "Imagine

you could fly to the moon." Flying to the moon was no problem. Grant felt exhilarated and split. Even as part of his mind cast for visual images to depict the words of the song, another part tried to consider the budget, imagining the possibilities for incredible equipment—a crane, a chopper. At first he thought he might take a crew to Paris and shoot the whole thing there. He imagined scenes at the Eiffel Tower. But, when he called her at the company in the morning to try out this idea, he found that he'd been unrealistic. Maybe he could shoot a solo act in Paris, she told him gently, but, as there were four guys in the Greenberry Woods, the cost might be prohibitive. In the end they would shoot the music video on a soundstage in Burbank, the set simulating Paris with cobblestones, a Gothic arch, and traveling mattes of France.

Grant worked from some surreal images by the painter René Magritte. In one image a man looked into a mirror, while from the back of his head, another image of his face looked out. Two of the Greenberry Woods were identical twins, and Grant could recreate this painting easily enough. Other Magritte images attracted him, too, all of them in the surrealist manner incorporating incongruous imagery to strange effect. In one, the outline of a man in a derby enclosed a landscape of trees in the china blue light of evening. The new moon shone where his forehead might have been. In others, a large green apple obscured a businessman's face; glasses of water fell from the sky; four Italian cypress trees seemed to step from the surface of a painting. Grant wrote variations of these images into his treatment, incorporating them with the lyrics of the song. He'd been told to fly to the moon, and so he was.

In the treatment conference, the record company people especially liked the image of the four Italian cypress trees emerging from the canvas. It was a good gag, they said, and in the end they'd given him the go-ahead. Grant was delighted, so happy to be connected with this company, though not quite realizing at that point that a gun had gone off, so to speak, that the race to produce the video was on.

The Greenberry Woods had two guitars, drums, and bass, like the Beatles. They had the early Fab Four's skiffle style as well: boppy and lyrical with harmonies in the chorus. Like Grant, the Greenberry Woods had achieved an initial success—they'd done one video already, though just a simple one, of concert scenes lighted and shot at a club in New York. Like Grant, they were just now getting the full treatment for the first time. They were young, all four about twenty-two. Grant was twenty-eight.

The company faxed Grant's treatment to them while they were on tour. It reached them in Chicago at the Vic Theater. For their tour, the band had been wearing black jackets and black jeans and various pastel T-shirts. Grant's idea of putting them in turn-of-the-century suits and Magritte-style bowlers appealed to them.

Also they were psyched to go back to LA. From their homes in Baltimore they'd be flying across the country for the shoot. They'd been out there once before, when their album *Rappledapple* had just come out, and the band had performed from a flatbed truck, parked in front of the company.

For the story, the band posed one problem. Each of the four members of the band needed equal time in the video, as they were—again, like the Beatles—a four-part personality, Matt, Brandt, Miles, and Ira, each equally attractive and interesting. Though in the song only one guy said adieu to just one girl, in the video the girl had to say good-bye to all four guys. To Grant, it couldn't be a sexual thing, with all of them involved like that. So he wrote it as four farewells among friends.

Grant was out of his body, as he put it, from his first moment of waking that first day, so hyped up he wouldn't know it for weeks. He spent that day touring production houses, surprised to see that they had no sets or cameras in their offices, just telephones and a conference room. Production houses contracted the vendors, provided the insurance, acted as the legal entity. In this first series of meetings, Grant and the record company executive interviewed candidates, choosing the production house, and then the producer and the director of photography and all the other people who would work on the project.

In these meetings, Grant sat quietly. Being new, he knew none of these people, of course, and so he was listening carefully, trying to take it in, the terminology constantly defying his understanding. At the end of these meetings an awful lull would impose itself, during which Grant would get the alarming feeling that he, as the director, was supposed to say something. In the first one, with a candidate for producer, he said—as a courtesy—"I'd be glad to work with you," and instantly it was so.

The two-week whirlwind spiraled toward the shoot. Grant blasted around the freeways, panicky, trying to remember everything. On the set he was suddenly in charge, everyone looking to him as the guy who'd made it up. Immersed in details, he could barely spare the moment to take pleasure in having his will done. He had to keep moving, allowing himself only a second to survey the scene at the soundstage, to marvel to himself at this intent crew of professionals racing to build the five sets his storyboard required.

Several of the shots he'd outlined, it turned out, demanded blue screens. For a scene of The Girl in Paris, in which her image would be imposed over the moving images of the streets of the city, the model would move in front of a blue screen and the scene would be shot on blue-sensitive film, a process that would allow her image to be superimposed on the images of the streets. Grant had also conceived some of the images in his film as themselves pictures in an art gallery, so on one of the sets the workers first erected an enormous blue screen, thirty by forty feet, and then built a huge picture frame around it. Come to learn, he said in his laconic Texan way, that most music videos are blue screens.

Grant found a costumer named Delphime and was pleased by the coincidence of her French name, though at first her suits didn't match, as he had requested. Then the art department informed him that actual water in the glasses that fell from the sky wouldn't work. Actual water would slosh.

The number of things on his daily list doubled, then tripled. Then he had no time for anything, was still and would be out of his body. The three days he needed to shoot became two, and rushed down upon him.

On the first day of shooting, Grant worked on location in a house with a guerrilla crew: a couple of guys, the model who played The Girl, a shiny board, and a camera. He managed. It was pretty easy, actually, though they'd saved all the hard stuff for the next day. When the crew shouted, "We need The Girl now," The Girl came on.

Grant also met the Greenberry Woods that first day, in the parking lot. They arrived in a limo from the fancy hotel where the studio had put them—the Mondrian, where the bathrooms were gridded and touched with details in primary colors, the soaps in gels of green and red, like Mondrian's paintings. Getting out of the limo, the band seemed young to Grant. They talked to him about what they wanted to do in the video, though by then Grant wasn't fazed. He'd seen the soundstage, after all, the vast production that had come of his sketches, the workers and highly technical equipment and lights, the Sensurround speakers for the song. Once the Greenberry Woods got on the soundstage, Grant knew they'd feel tiny, too. They'd be praying for someone to give them directions.

Afterward, Grant felt that the band members were probably nice guys, and wished he had gotten to know them. Just at that moment in the parking lot, though, they had to get fitted for their suits and derbies, and the next time he saw them, they were all at sea in the emergency of the shoot.

The soundstage was, for one thing, deafeningly loud. During the shoot, the sound system powered the song "Adieu" down at them, its din drowning—barely—the roar of the other machines. Grant couldn't have imagined that as a director he'd actually have to shout at the top of his lungs and still not be heard. He didn't know, also, that he couldn't just yell "Action!" because action requires a blank space, a leader, an upbeat, if it is to begin in unison. So Grant's first shout threw everybody for a loop, until the director of photography, solicitously, killingly, said, "It might be better if you said, 'And . . . Action!'" So Grant went to film school on the spot, what he didn't know dawning on everyone.

After a while the assistant director offered to do the shouting. His voice would carry better, he said. But in one early shot—an easy one, it would turn out—in which the band had simply to walk, single file, like the Beatles on the Abbey Road cover, moving their feet, of course, to the tempo of their song, the AD whose voice could carry couldn't get the beat, and the band needed the direction. Grant tried it over and over—the DP pleading for him to cut and save film—until he finally had to go up himself, just off camera, and bellow at these four young men from Baltimore in their matching wool suits and derbies, who walked single file like the Beatles for take after take until they got it. This for an early, easy shot.

A table loaded with food appeared mysteriously on the set. Grant couldn't remember ordering it, though it proved providential as the shoot went on and on, and suppertime came, and then so soon afterward it was midnight under the hot lights, everyone bleary-eyed and greasy, and Grant still trying to make four Italian cypress trees appear to emerge, doing take after fruitless take, as the DP, a pro who'd done a shoot like this a million times, let him know they were running out of film, and still had three storyboards to go.

In the end the trees wouldn't work. They just wouldn't work, and Grant pushed and pushed, determined that, at the very least, everyone would see that it wouldn't work, technically. By then he was grimly grateful to have them there, as witnesses.

*T*hen, the next day, in the cold light of the first edit, he couldn't see it, as hard as he tried, and the low resolution of the working tape was only half the problem. Looking at the pixelized proceedings on the soundstage, Grant could no longer tell if the images told the story of the song. Every image was overloaded with meaning. He had to call a friend who was a stranger to the whole process, and ask him to come down to the studio and then just watch the tape, so that he could return to his own sense of listening to the song and seeing those images for the first time. This worked. Watching his friend watching the tape, Grant could instantly see it himself again. He did the edit and sent the tape to the record company.

The next day in the on-line studio, they simply put a floppy disk into a bay and let it code and edit the film. Then he could see the work in brilliant, 35-millimeter images, so clear it looked as if you could walk into them, Grant said. Looking at these images, Grant was horrified. The worst was the technical failure of some of the blue screens. The Girl had been too near the screen, it turned out, and the blue light—barely reflected in patches on her face and shoulders—allowed the superimposed image, the Parisian street scene, to play there like a chaotic tattoo. He hadn't been able to see this on the fuzzy digital tape, which had already gone to the record company, but here on this superclear film, it shrieked. He had to throw it out. He had to throw a bunch of stuff out. Among other things, the whole last, awful, three hours on the soundstage had been wasted. So he had to make do with what he had, putting the final edit together.

Grant was further shocked, then, to see how long this little three-and-a-half-minute song turned out to be—an eternity, when an image appearing in a music video for a single second was too long. The piece needed dozens of images, a storyboard twice as long as the one he had designed. As it was, he didn't even have half the images he'd planned, what with the kill rate from the soundstage. So he had to repeat images. Now, when he watches MTV, he notices that repetition and knows what happened, a little song swallowing pictures like a whale surfacing through krill.

He felt crushed, but he finished the piece, unable to stop thinking about how awful this was for the record company, which had been brave enough to take a risk, to place such faith in him. In the end, though, the executive called to say that she thought it was OK. It worked. In the end "Adieu" got air. "Adieu, adieu, adieu, adieu," the boys sang. "Goodbye to you."

About that time, Grant saw *The Color Purple* again, and could only look with envy and amazement at Spielberg's lingering takes. MTV seemed as different from movies, after that, as movies were from books. The guy just ran and ran the camera.

For a while, Grant wasn't sure what to do next. Then the lead singer for the Jayhawks asked him to shoot a film for a song he'd written. The singer, Mark, wanted to pay for the production himself. The song was a ballad about his father's suicide. By then Grant knew, at least, what not to do. With Mark and his friend Victoria and their dog Molly, he drove up into the Mojave Desert around Joshua Tree, taking along just his old Super 8. He had an idea of emptiness and beyond that, nothing. He intended to wing it.

Emerging on the desert plateau, they'd found clouds, puffs of white that Grant had seen in Texas, though not often in California, separate cumulus bundles—as if on order—drifting across the blue of the desert sky. Then from the road, they'd spotted an old house on a hilltop, and later on a whim decided to go back and check it out, scrambling up the rocks to reach the gate.

Inside, broken glass was strewed across the floor, appearing as chunks of reflected light. The stove lay off its moorings. In what seemed like the child's room, they found torn wallpaper, patterned with hearts. The western light was drawing to horizontal, just then, and they decided to hurry up and shoot film before somebody came to throw them out or arrest them. They had a single prop, a small, battered suitcase. Mark and Victoria sang the song and acted it out, and Grant just ran and ran the camera, until he ran out of film. That night the three of them and the dog Molly found a cheap motel in Pioneertown.

The Cloud of Unknowing

Umberto Eco, for one, suggests that the Middle Ages ended in the thirteenth century when the scholastic Robert Grosseteste, in his groundbreaking experiments with optics, made a firm distinction between hallucination and sight. Before that the Middle Ages had proceeded in a universe of hallucination, writes Eco in his essay on Thomas Aquinas.

Maybe blue-screening, morphing, special effects, Photoshopping, the making real of impossible images, maybe these technical advances herald a reverse flow, back to an epoch of visual iconography and collective hallucination, a return to "the symbolic forest peopled with mysterious presences," that Eco says characterized the earlier age. Or maybe we don't have to go back, to get there.

At the party I met a saxophonist who also managed a stock photo business during the day. At night, he played tenor and soprano saxes in various bands. He seemed conversant with a variety of styles—big band, rockabilly, New Orleans rhythm and blues—all the strands of twentieth-century American music, it seemed. We talked about Duke Ellington, though he played the Neville Brothers. Then the topic turned to his day job.

His stock agency brokered photographs, selling the one-time use of an image to corporate clients who used them in brochures and advertising. The agency library had thousands of files—pictures in categories such as "Nature," "Food," "People"—with hundreds of images of couples, for instance, subclassed under "People," and in a further subcategory, couples posed in every kind of kiss.

These files kept growing, of course. The agency took in new photos all the time, as the up-to-dateness of its imagery was part of the basis for its reputation. The photographers brought in their new shots. Historically, he told me, stock photo agencies had tried to offer the clients the images that they already had in mind, differing in this aim from photojournalism, say. So each new picture needed to sustain a recognizable gesture though recloaking it in the objects and people and circumstances of the present moment.

Things were changing in the stock photo business, he told me. For one thing, it was getting wired. Its new thing was on-line art, those images digitized, placed on the information superhighway, and broadcast worldwide for personal use. You'd be able to develop your own pictorial lexicon from a huge palette of images at your fingertips, to build your own up-to-the-moment icon bank, including the kissing couple of your choice.

Among the categories of pictures he mentioned was one called "Concepts." This pleased me, just then, to think of "Concepts" as simply one more category, "Concepts" along with "Food," like jazz along with funk. Maybe there was hope. What kind of pictures were in the "Concepts" file, I wondered.

Dollar bills on fire, it turned out, a lighted door at the end of a darkened hallway, a dart stuck in a bull's-eye, hands holding a globe, a road under the stars.

The Gate of Arcesilaus

David Hume was a skeptic and a good fat fellow in an age of gentleman. He was the younger son of a Scottish noble family, and so had to seek his own fortune, at first disastrously in law, and then with preposterous success in rational philosophy—preposterous because it proved surprisingly lucrative and because Hume himself knew that he was never quite at home reasoning. Though Hume trumped the Cartesians, the shape of his life argues that the reasonableness of one's conclusions doesn't ultimately matter, but that something else does, some older, effortless, unreasoning assurance. His nature, he called it. That reason is and ought only to be the slave of the passions is his famous maxim. More tellingly, he wrote, "we assent to our faculties and employ our reason only because we cannot help it."

"Our Davie," Hume's mother is reputed to have said of him, "is a fine good-natured creature, but uncommon weak-minded." She was perhaps simply being maternal and covering for his scandalous atheism by impugning his faculties. Though in no ordinary sense weak-minded, Hume was strange. In his short autobiography he wrote that he was "absolutely and necessarily determined to live and talk and act like other people in the common affairs of life." Of course to pledge oneself to normality is itself abnormal, though in Hume's case he had no choice. His strangeness, his Olympian "weak-mindedness" led him reasonably to conclude that much of what other people took to be the granite foundations of reality were transparent habits of mind and unwarranted, empirically speaking.

In the matter of detaching philosophy from God, Hume's best ally turned out to be Berkeley, who as a bishop of the Church had done the brunt of the work. Attacking rationalist assumptions of equivalence between objects in reality and their representations in mind, Berkeley had obligingly deconstructed matter, collapsing it into the other elements of Locke's epistemological universe—the mind, ideas, and God.

Hume said that most of Berkeley's writings "form the best lessons of skepticism," praise that would have horrified Berkeley himself. If, as Berkeley had suggested, the external world of matter could not be empirically tested against its mental counterparts, neither could much else. Hume extended Berkeley's critique, collapsing all the elements of Locke's catalogue into chaos, into a realm in which a mind without reasonable justification for its own existence perceived a world similarly unfounded, in events that themselves could yield no causal relationship to one another.

Ockham's and Berkeley's first cause, God, was no exception. God could not be reasoned into existence. "Nothing could set in a fuller light the infinite obligations which mankind have to Divine revelation," Hume wrote, "since we find that no other medium could ascertain this great and important truth." Even this his publisher at first refused to print. God could be explained, said Hume in an essay published posthumously, as a manifestation of the "tendency among mankind to conceive all beings like themselves, and to transfer to every object those qualities with which they are familiarly acquainted."

Hume thought that previous philosophy had proceeded "without following steadily a chain of propositions." After Berkeley, Hume followed such a chain to withdraw rational justification from all the verities that the West had come to, by the Age of Reason. Hume, as much as anyone, delivered us into modern uncertainty.

Imagine descending into the chasm of habit, as if on one of those helicopter tours of the Grand Canyon. The topmost layers are what we glean from the new, the select events noticed among all that happens in the present moment, and of these just the rare one salient enough to connect to a pattern of ostensibly similar events in what we call the past. Beneath these lie our formulae, those connected events one carries consciously, little histories of trials and errors, some effective, some—like tomato juice on airplanes—simply invoking luck, a wish that outward circumstance will have its inner correspondence, as the appearance of a dove might augur peace. Deeper still are the unconscious assumptions, embedded in linguistic structures and influencing the subtle choices—not even recognized as choices—that we make previous to perceiving anything.

In Hume's graceful periodic sentences, one views the depths, the most basic of human assumptions—of cause and effect, consistency in oneself, the feeling of time, of a future gathering in this moment, a past somehow accumulated both as personal memory and as "all our belief in history." All these, for Hume, are mental constructs, the mind's boxes, and reality beyond a fabulous wraith washing us with images, no two alike.

Naturally Hume saw himself likewise. "When I enter most intimately into what I call *myself*," he wrote, "I always stumble on some particular perception or other, of heat or cold, light or shade, love or hatred, pain or pleasure." Such a self was a creature of everything and nothing, and of language, in Hume's case of careful, courteous, eighteenth-century English sentences, their clauses anyway always wending home.

How did Hume do, living as such a creature and having arrived at such conclusions? Just fine, thank you very much. This portly man—his figure, said a contemporary, better suited to a turtle-eating alderman than a refined philosopher—had a gift for fitting in. He could leave his philosophical self behind, he wrote, when he played backgammon with his friends. That his reasoning self had proceeded into a void of philosophical uncertainty didn't seem to matter.

He had a "sanguine temper," Hume explained, invoking perhaps unconsciously the medieval theory of the humors to explain this ability to take his ease among his fellow men, to be cordial and resilient in spite of his reasoned and enormous conclusions about the "imperfections and narrow limits of human understanding."

"Philosophy would render us entirely Pyrrhonian," he wrote, "were not nature too strong for it." Pyrrho of Elis, who wrote nothing, was the first systematic skeptic. Hume was, by contrast, the first author in history to become rich from the sales of his books. He knew where he lived no matter what he thought. "Carelessness and inattention alone can afford us any remedy," he said. "For this reason I entirely rely upon them."

This unbeliever died in that year of our independence, 1776, expiring in bestseller opulence and, to all eyes, in peace, speaking with affection and tenderness to his friends and, rationally alert to his demise, dismissing their faint hopes as groundless. Boswell came to Hume's bedside and reported afterward to Dr. Johnson that Hume seemed to view the prospect of his death with serenity. The rock-kicking Christian doctor insisted that Hume was faking it.

Hume seems, though, to have retained his humor to the end. Adam Smith, another deathbed witness, wrote in a letter that Hume continued to display the irony that had led him to his metaphysical discoveries in the first place. Suffering little pain, he read Lucian's *Dialogues of the Dead* and reported that he found himself with none of the excuses that the dying usually offer to Charon to delay getting aboard his ferry to the underworld. I have a house to finish; I have a grievance to revenge; I have a child to raise, they say. But Hume has none of these, and what he imagines offering to the dark boatman, Charon easily refutes. I have some corrections for the new edition, he says.

There is no end to editing, the ultimate editor replies.

But I've not yet opened the eyes of the public, pleads Hume, adding, "if I live a few years longer, I may have the satisfaction of seeing the downfall of some of the prevailing systems of superstition."

"Get into this boat this instant," Charon shouts, "you lazy, loitering rogue."

Partial skepticism—a struggling against suckholes—enervates us, induces despair. But here was Hume's secret: A monastic renunciation of the mind's capacity to establish ultimate truth could be enlivening, rejuvenating. That such full surrender to doubt swung open the gate of Arcesilaus, the Platonic skeptic who concluded that "Nothing is certain, not even that." And beyond that gate stretched everything, the whole wide realm of possibility.

And what of God, from whom after Hume philosophy would veer? Abandoned by Western empirical thought—image the slight—God might well go on anyway, persisting with everything else in a universe where even uncertainty was uncertain, persisting, maybe, as Berkeley and Ockham had imagined him, as the source behind the flickering images of life as we perceive it, as the light of Genesis even, cast westward though the halls and alcoves of Solomon's Temple, Notre Dame, Rockefeller Center, Universal Studios, as our destiny, our offering, even as divine will expressed in whatever happens next.

Or perhaps God's gift was his departure. Skepticism's ef-

fect, said Hume, was "momentary amazement and irresolution." Such doubt might be a zimzum, a suspension of
preconception in the midst of an intractably unreasonable
existence, which even such as Hume managed to live as if
assuredly. Pure doubt might provide a point of nowhere, of
nothing, from which one might behold it all.

The Eye of Jupiter

By the end of the party, the end of that night, and that long day in LA, one thing was clear. I had failed in my quest. I was finding my own mind everywhere. I wasn't postmodern, I wasn't modern, I was still medieval. Even my little Copernican fantasy, that I might perceive the turning earth, acknowledge the scientific facts, assume the actual scale, hadn't held. I couldn't be actual, not for more than a minute, anyway.

As midnight arrived at the party, I knew this and felt drowsed, as if under the spell of the whole day's thinking. With the desperation of the tired, I began to devise a way to go home or—as I had no home in LA—at least to somewhere like it. Leaving at all wouldn't be easy, as we didn't have a car, and even leaving gracefully might be unlikely. The party was still in full swing. The host had left an hour earlier, to go to another gathering, and on leaving had asked me to stay until he got back. Sure, I'd said, though by then I didn't feel as if I could. I decided to find Les.

During that year of my life, I had been thinking of her rather consciously as "my friend," as a way of holding some older meaning in abeyance. Part of being with her, I'd come to appreciate, meant not acting as a unit all the time, which she said not only didn't mean that you didn't care, but evidenced that you did. Honestly I did not know at this point, and "friend" seemed a roomy enough relation to hold what it was. What it was probably had to go unnamed, though as a feeling it still had power over me. How could such a specific, potent, intimate thing suddenly become anonymous? I thought. I needed a name—this was another way I had failed to be new. I made my way through the loud crowd at the party, looking for her. Where was she?

I'd noticed her around the party at various points during the evening, as at various points in the day, which we'd spent among others in groups that had included us, but in which we'd spoken outwardly, to these LA people. We were the visitors, and so hadn't spoken to each other much. But enough absence, I was thinking by then, happy to seek her out, there at the end of the evening, for three private words.

I found her by the window, those sycamore branches now stirring beyond the panes. She was talking with a tall, curly-haired woman named Carissa, whom I'd met earlier. The three of us chatted until Carissa, providentially as it were, mentioned that she had to go home. Then in the moment after Carissa turned to depart, I leaned toward Les, and, close to her ear, asked, "Want to leave?"

She'd had a long day, too, and seemed grateful that I'd asked. She did, she said.

We still had to arrange it. I caught up with Carissa and asked if we could get a ride, and Les checked with Jess who said sure, no problem, and gave us her key to the apartment. At the door, I said goodnight and thanks to Tracy and feeling sheepish asked her to convey my regrets to Bruce for not sticking around. Then I followed Carissa and Les down the stairs and out into the dark, where the breeze rustled above us. We walked the deserted sidewalk to her car.

Carissa drove the broad square blocks, smoothing the corners on the diagonal and sure of her route. When she let us out, we entered the dark apartment tentatively. The key turned with difficulty in the unfamiliar lock, and the furniture required negotiation. I felt for the light switch.

Then, before we could sleep in it, we had to make the study into a bedroom by putting the futon down and making it up as a bed. Tired, we stood at each end of this Japanese couch and pulled out its wooden plugs, slid open the shellacked hinged frame, then flattened the heavy, pliant mattress and made it up western style with the fitted sheets and quilt that Jess had left out for us.

Even these penultimate acts—midnight past now—seemed emblematic to my tired mind. I folded my white pants over the chair where the purple shorts still hung on the arm. The motives of the day, or at least my need to find motives in the day, lingered, despite or because of my tiredness. A sound mind tolerates a mystery, I had read somewhere. So much for that. I said goodnight to my friend by her name, like a friend, though she kissed me anyway—or maybe because—and I had a moment of wondering if I could also tell her about this day with its epochal train of thought that had borne me off like the TGV. That moment was, though, momentary. I never heard Jess and Steve come in.

I knew almost nothing about Jupiter, in my dream. I drove my car out into the countryside, worrying about it. I could recall only a few precious facts: It was freezing there, it had moons of ice; it was huge, of course, its horizon appearing concave in the Jovian gravity. There was lots of color, though I couldn't recall any specific hues. A vast storm, like an eye on its titanic face, had stood locked open since the Middle Ages. Also—personally speaking—I couldn't stand it there for a second, so heavy that my own body would crush my bones.

What I knew about Jupiter was over in an instant, and I could just see myself up there in front of those country people, silent and sure that more would follow. Why Jupiter? I said aloud in the car. Why hadn't I paid more attention?

At last, out of the fields, the town rose, turning out to be just buildings at a crossroads. On the corner stood two young women. I rolled down the window. I'm giving a lecture on Jupiter, I said. The planet, not the god.

Oh, we know where that is, said one of the women.

And don't worry, said the other. Just say what you always say.

Day

Ante Meridiem

In the early light of Sunday morning, before we got up to go to the beach, as my friend slept on beside me on the futon, I had decided what the heck, I'd be medieval. I'd been amusing myself for a while by studying the bookshelf, which took up most of the wall beyond the bed. Jess and Steve had movie books, books about the making of films, books on how to write scripts. They had literature, too, from several centuries and countries. Some of these books they had no doubt sought out and read avidly, some had probably been required in courses, some had maybe been given as gifts, intended for them by others.

I'd always liked pondering bookshelves, trying to let the collection indicate its whole personality, the obvious and odd books, the worn and the unread, the decorative and the workaday, the meaningful and the accidental all making a kind of chord, as on an elaborate pipe organ. But that morning, I knew whose chord this was, finally—my own. I couldn't assume then that the total effect had only to do with Jess and Steve, or even with the books themselves. I had my own favorites among the titles and also other unavoidable associations, not to mention large areas of unknowing, for that matter. I composed my version of the bookshelves, this in the midst of the larger description of my moment that I composed all the time, creating my cosmos.

That was the bookshelf, the moment that I had. I recalled Galileo in my drowned book denying that we might perceive the earth's motion directly. Fixed to the planet, he'd said, we shared its every movement. The sky would always seem to turn. This was the essential medieval thing, that I assumed the world, moving toward it from my own intentions, from my names for it. The underlying premise, that one's own position was universal, that one's meaning *was* the world, this was the main flow, it seemed, and the modern moment had been but an eddy.

So I'd failed in my thinking. So be it, I thought. I'd be medieval, if that's what I was. I'd embrace it. Maybe I had seen life in chiaroscuro for a moment, as it were, but that was over. Now it was back to local color, flat perspective. In medieval tapestry, these devices had insisted in their way on significance, of the color and of each object. Then in the modern moment had come shadings and perspective, chiaroscuro and the vanishing point, reminding us that color changes depending on the light and that objects relate according to point of view.

And now these pixels, these icons and stars, the focus-grouped segments of the marketplace, the discrete channels and local constituencies—these bits and blips, anyway, again presented each color for its own sake. This development could seem exacting about every separate thing, at least at first, before our sense of the whole faded, before we lost the knack of seeing things as if from the outside.

But this was my time; this was the field of folk, and I was among them. Since I was, I'd be some local color myself. I'd make myself a monk of my own order, a pilgrim on my own path. I'd go with it, like everybody else rendering my impulses into a system with its own gravity, as it were, seating myself at the center of my own crystal sphere, where I might hearken unto its music, hymns to the God who had created me in his own image, conveniently enough.

So be it then. It wasn't as if I'd have to get robes and a tonsure. I could get up, shower, put those medieval shorts on, and go forth into LA, to the beach. I leaned my medieval chin against my friend's shoulder. I hadn't seen her enough, that weekend, and I was hoping to wake her up, though she wouldn't. It must still be early, I thought, feeling resolved. Outside somewhere a bird sang, and I let it sing for me.

For a couple of hours after that, I ate bagels and drank coffee and lounged around the dining room table with the others, the sections of the Sunday LA *Times* parceled out among us. When I returned to the bedroom to pack up our few belongings, I took my white pants off the chair, folded them up and put them in my bag. I found my book on the floor, still open to the "Triumph of Secularism." As I'd hoped it had dried beneath the window, the tomato fibers now crusty in the fold. I sat down and rubbed the affected pages, raking the fibers with my hand into the wastebasket, the dry tomato flaking to fuzz almost, and leaving pink dust briefly in the air. The text emerged on a field now simply tinted yellow, as with age. The book had been thickened in the way of a summer novel engulfed by a sneaker wave. It wouldn't close fully. I felt friendly toward it just then, though I couldn't say why. Its tomato juice bath had warped it weirdly.

That morning we were off to the beach for the day, from there to head for the airport for a five o'clock flight home. The beach was a welcome prospect, as always. Its broad, fluid body, the coast finite by comparison, and even the sand on the beach had always suggested the Beyond to me. The idea of spending the day there lightened everything. I might not be modern. Secularism wasn't triumphing. But the beach might still hold its promise.

We folded the linens and put the bed back up, transforming it into a couch again and the room into a study. I checked to make sure I'd left nothing in the room. Then with the small ceremony of briefly saying good-bye to the cat, who endured this with no concept of good-bye herself, we left. I put on those Wayfarers again and carried our luggage out into bright sunshine, stowing the bags in the trunk of the rented Pontiac, which was still at the curb where we'd left it the morning before. It was warm and beautiful out, the metal surfaces already hot to the touch.

When I started the Pontiac, we didn't have to search for the music. The jazz station I had chosen the morning before was still on the radio. A sax trio came on with the ignition, doing an airy jazz waltz. We listened as we waited for Jess and Steve's Jetta to emerge from the garage behind their apartment. Having spoken to the sax player the night before, I had a new association with jazz sax in LA, and I imagined how—if I'd lived there—I might accumulate my own version of the town, associating it bit by bit like this, until I had created my own self-referenced LA, the little sphere in which I was no longer a visitor. For a half-second this made me feel slightly claustrophobic.

I followed Steve down Santa Monica Boulevard and across West LA toward the beach. Where La Cienega ran through the Baldwin Hills, the country felt open for a moment and original, the hills seeming somehow out of the Stone Age, the haunts of the woolly mammoth and the saber-toothed tiger. Oil pumps dipping on the hills there oddly enhanced this, like huge, affirmative, prehistoric black birds, bending their mechanical heads to drink.

For its very survival, life on earth had always proceeded on its own terms. Why should human beings be any different, I was thinking. Because they had the capacity to wonder about it? So what? What good did that do, after all? Maybe consciousness itself had been an evolutionary mistake, an adaptation that hadn't worked out. Whatever, nobody could for sure say why life occurred, though even shrugging demonstrated the fact that it had and did. Nod, nod, nod, without knowledge. A man thinks and God laughs, was the Yiddish proverb. Maybe a man from the Middle Ages would find this funny, too.

In his green Jetta, Steve picked up the 405 and went past the airport exit. Flowering bushes erupted from the shoulders of the freeway, poisonous oleanders and red bottle-brushy trees and bougainvillea, which seemingly flourished in the hot wind of the traffic. After a mile or so, he signaled and took Rosecrans, that avenue rising dead west and cresting the last hill, from which I could not see the beach and the broad blue horizon that morning, obscured as they were by the fringe of the ocean fog.

Wider than a Mile

A palm tree, with a severed yellow and brown palm frond lying at its base on the street near the curb—this too could seem a kind of icon. The new fronds had sprouted from the top of the trunk, raising the tree's crown and shading the old ones from direct sunlight. Each old frond had fallen as this one had, withered, weakened, until some breeze or accident had finally severed it, the frond broken off close to the trunk, its ragged base remaining. So the trunk was thatched with stubs from such old breakage, those precise moments memorialized in the pattern of fibrous cross-sections that spiraled up the tree. This record of breakage was the great gesture of the tree's growth, as, frond by frond, the palm had raised its feathery green head into the wind.

I let this tree's meaning, its poignancy for time-stranded

me, be its first reality, its significance seeming to bear its actuality, rather than the other way around. I tried to feel this pull as a kind of psychic gravity on that foggy morning. The long trunk leaned inland, trained that way on previous days when the ocean breeze had blown.

So I proceeded through my meanings and personal associations, through this neighborhood of bungalows, toward the beach. We'd parked a little inland, quite near the house of my cousin Cynthia. I had stayed at Cynthia's a few years before, on that occasion going into the surf on her teenage son's boogie board. Cynthia was a second-generation descendent of that Alabaman family whose sons and daughters—my mother excepted—had raised their families all over LA, those descendants now spread, as in Genesis, like grains of sand upon the shore, from Ventura to Orange County.

During the summer that she was sixteen, Cynthia had come back east to stay with my family. She was a freckled strawberry blonde who'd seemed a southern Californian goddess to me then. I was about twelve at the time, and followed her around, amazed, as she sunned at the local pool and at home played her records by Henry Mancini and His Orchestra and the Ray Conniff Singers. She went on dates—this had resonated for me, having no older siblings myself—she went on dates, even, to Georgetown with the lifeguards, who were almost eighteen.

So walking downhill with Les and Jess and Steve, I could sing "Moon River" to myself as if that melody—and all that past—were part of the physical atmosphere I was passing through, as if the song had hung there all those years, waiting for me to walk by, no different from the radio's staying tuned to that jazz station all day Saturday, while the car had sat parked at the curb.

We walked the few blocks to the beach, first into a little inland valley, where the train track had run. Its right-of-way had been transformed into a greenbelt with jogging track, even this little park emblematic of the whole history of the American West, the coming and going of the railroad. We proceeded safari-style with our beach stuff, mounting the narrow street beyond. At the top I could see the last far west bit of America, the houses getting nicer and nicer the nearer the beach. Overhead the fog's wispy edge was dissolving, though the beach below was still shrouded in mist.

Gardens fronted many of the houses, roses especially abundant among them in the moist sea air, and every blossom seemed to call to Les and Jess, who shared an obsession with flowers. Steve and I were carrying collapsible short-legged chairs, a blanket and towels, the food, clothes, and books, but the women had to pause to admire the flowers, to put their faces to the blooms, to stop, without irony even, and smell the roses. Finally Steve and I had to stop, too. Look at this lantana, you guys, Jess had said. So I did, smelling for a moment its tiny purple clusters. Then we tried to press ahead over the sandy pavement, though the women continued to be diverted, exclaiming at each new eruption of flowers, even chatting up one of the gardeners, who paused in her gloves and visor and looked up, happy to hear their praise for the vegetation.

$\mathcal{H}$alfway down the hill, we crossed the main beach road, entirely beneath the fog now and into its chill, from there proceeding between the truly fantabulous houses, coming down to the twin terraces of the paved boardwalks—one for walkers, another for the silent, speeding nonmotorized conveyances called bicycles—then descending the steps onto the sand. On the broad beach, a few volleyballers were already playing, thudding the ball around in those halt triplets of set-up and spike. They played in bikinis, women and men, and their highly muscled, bronzed near-nudity was like perfect flesh, southern Californian hard bodies of the new type. They had definition. They wore such meaning, they were such meaning, that I wondered if they could ever feel naked, if they would strip simply to their logos, where that would be that.

It was refreshing, then, to turn to the broad empty beach, the vast sea, in contrast to which the isolated lifeguard's hut on its stilts seemed pleasantly momentary, liable to be cast adrift in the next big storm, its ramshackle quality essentially, wackily human. Even the Italianate Manhattan Beach Pier, a quarter mile or so south in the mist, seemed pleasantly contingent, it too pressed against the elements, the waves breaking on the pilings beneath it, its decorative aspect seeming deployed as a charm against the sea.

The lifeguard shelter was locked up, deserted, and we walked past it to the tide's reach, the salt smell of the ocean intensifying. The last highest wave had left a margin of kelp and sea wrack, and beyond this the sand was still smooth from the nightly tide. Rehearsed in Newtonianism by then —for all the good it did me—I had to imagine the enormous mass of the moon plunging past in the bright dark of space and dragging this very water off the beach in its gravitational wake. Even the ocean fog had to do with the rolling earth, I recalled. Like a tablecloth pulled beneath a wine glass, the eastward-rolling land pulled away from the warm surface of the ocean. The cold depths rotated up to replace it at the shore, and, lifted into warm wind, made the fog. That seemed actual enough, though by then these were icons as well, merely representing actuality to my medieval mind.

We made our beach camp on top of the little bluff the waves had cut in soft sand. On that last dry, flat area we spread out our blanket and towels and unpacked our things. My friends had their bathing suits on underneath their clothes—I planned to swim in my medieval shorts—but nobody made a move to take anything off in the foggy chill. The women lay on their stomachs on the blanket, their arms folded beneath them as they talked, and Steve and I sat in the folding chairs, got out books, and leaned back to look up into the fog. Up there a ghostly, mottled sun wavered. We had seen it like this before, though. It was just a matter of time, Steve said.

I studied the waves, scrying them. That day the dominant swell was southerly. The best waves were running four or five feet, maybe, but were mostly closed out—not peeling neatly, but falling over all at over. A weaker swell from the northwest cut these dominant impulses, tripping the longer lines into sections. I imagined this insinuation of northwesterly swell becoming explicit as winter came on, until some January storm would turn wheels of foam out of that quadrant, commanding the beach.

Just then the broad plaid surface signified September. Once in a while a big southerly set would assert itself. These waves, a foot or two larger, gathered the sections for a longer break, like the last pulses of the summer. Down by the pier, two short boarders and a boogie boarder, it looked like, were passing up the smaller sets, waiting on these.

The Tube

When I first heard about the paradox that matter could consist of either particles or waves, depending on which you chose to perceive, I knew I'd choose waves. Particles seemed boring. The apparent palpability of waves, combined with the mystery that what manifested a wave remained afterward as before, and most of all, with the feeling that I, as matter, consisted of waves myself, that my solidity too was a manifestation of invisible energies, this thrilled me.

My enthusiasm derived, of course, from surf. I'd learned to bodysurf as a kid on the beaches of LA, then was exiled to the East for my teen years. In northern Virginia, I met a guy who had moved there from Hawaii, where he'd surfed the North Shore, a claim that glorified him among our friends.

The next summer on a ten-foot Gordon Smith I'd tried to ride the warm wash of the eastern sea at Indian River Inlet and Assateague and Virginia Beach and Nag's Head, without much success. In those waves, riding that big board was like surfing on a phone pole.

That winter we crossed the icy Potomac on a regular pilgrimage into the district to see *The Endless Summer*. The surf documentary played at the Janus I, a tiny art house in Dupont Circle, and ran for about six months, into the spring. We went almost every weekend, vicariously on that quest for the perfect wave.

By the next winter, I was driving dates into town to the Janus II to see *A Man and a Woman*. It was over, for surf. At graduation my friend's parents offered him the choice between a trip to college and a trip back to Hawaii, to the North Shore of Oahu. He chose Hawaii, and has not yet returned. But I went on to college, to Buffalo yet, to read the Beats and William Carlos Williams.

Still, by then I'd acquired—for life—a detailed catalogue of ocean waves breaking on beaches I'd never actually seen. I had pictures in my head of the long crisp break at County Line, the Newport Beach Wedge, the big winter swell at Windansea, and dozens of other waves—just energy, after all, passing through the fluid matter of the sea, but powerful to me, gleaned from surf movies and the pages of surf magazines. I needed no caption or land features to identify a particular break. I knew these waves by color, shape, and size, and they would occur to me always, like icons to the anchorite, these variations on the tube, the perfect wave. These were my references, my book, whenever after I looked at the sea.

When I moved back to California as an adult, these pictures got me into trouble. I actually tried to get into big winter surf at La Jolla. I'd stood there on the rocks, in somebody else's wetsuit, holding a rented boogie board, watching long-boarders wait for an opening. With my own eyes, I'd seen the whole surface laden with foam from the swell breaking outside and even the shorebreak too big, gnarly and muscular. I'd seen veteran surfers hesitate before plunging in, then had clambered out myself onto the brink of a boulder, thinking it was now or never.

It was never, as it turned out. I remained in the water for two and a half waves, never seeing the other side of the third one. From the water, those waves looked like tumbling buses. The first knocked me off the boogie board. I had to dive beneath the next, emerging out of breath in the enormous face of the third one, which broke on me, took me in its grip and hurled me back a long way toward the rocks, miraculously driving me into a gap there, from which I crawled out of the sea, still attached by its tether to my Styrofoam toy, and pounded once or twice by those perfect waves, for good measure.

Having revered the original film, I was a little fearful going to see the sequel, which Bruce Brown put out twenty-five years later. I needn't have worried, it turned out, though of course some things had changed. The beach where Brown had found the first perfect wave has since then sprouted a housing development—in part because of the publicity for its perfect waves, no doubt. Pavement and foundations and sewer lines now anchor the sand there, so that it no longer replenishes the offshore bar, which in turn no longer plays its part in forming those waves, which now aren't perfect—at least in the way the movie intended.

Again the film follows the summer around the world, and again it proves endless, as Brown finds other perfect waves, some accessible only by skiff or helicopter. The new film is just as gee-whizzy as the first one, the jokes in Brown's voice-over every bit as corny. As in the first movie, Brown finds wild animals from which the surfers may flee for comic relief between surf spots. On the voice-over Brown thanks the audience, this too a holdover from his early days, when he would bring his silent surf footage to the beach-town theater himself and do the show live, as real waves broke in the dark a block away.

Still, I watched the remake, every moment, fascinated no matter what by waves. I could look at stones, to get a sense of eternity on earth. I could find a road cut into bedrock or go to the Grand Canyon and look down through the strata for billions of years. But rocks are heavy and difficult and ambiguous precisely because they don't seem to be, and I still prefer waves, which only seem to be bodiless, temporary. Waves are the earth's ancient gesture, the current and only moment. Of course everything is, but waves are so perfectly literal about it, their gesture consistent, their matter not their substance somehow.

In the new film there's a sequence recorded in the wave itself with a handheld, waterproof camera. Across the moving wall of water—by its bulk alone certainly the Pipeline—the surfer drops in, in slo-mo, as the wave goes critical, falls forward, throws out its thick top lip. The rider bottoms out, turns and climbs toward the camera, which submerges and through the clear tropical sea tracks him from below. The underside of his short board rips by, and from within the wave we watch him continue, out there on the wave in the bright thin element, where he intends to remain. For a few seconds, he finds that balance, has that control. Then the re-fracted form snaps and wavers, the lines of his wake dissolve, and that world collapses into fractals and blue.

The Manhattan
Beach Pier

Naturally, when one assumes a position, the evidence in opposition assumes one as well. That afternoon, despite—or because of—my medieval conclusion, something unexpected happened to counterbalance it. Against astronomical odds, I ran into Lloyd on the Manhattan Beach Pier. This small event, a random stroke of luck, reverberated through all my thinking that weekend, and released me from it. Though afterward I would remain a man of the Middle Ages, running into Lloyd would let me be medieval in something like the actual world.

By noon the fog had burned off, finally seeming to pop from the surface of the sea, and my mood had lifted by then, too. I'd ceased brooding and interpreting a little. By then I was lying on the blanket with the others, goofing around and debriefing the weekend, occasionally laughing at stuff

Jess said. Suddenly it was hot enough to sunbathe, and the horizon out to sea was a tight blue line. Dozens of encampments like ours now nested the bright beach, spaced at intervals in front of the lifeguard hut, which was inhabited now also, its flaps up and the white-nosed people gazing out from its shade. Kids had decided to wade, and were interjecting their shrieks into the waves. As it got hotter, some adults ventured in.

After a while we decided to walk to the pier to buy drinks. The women struck off first, heading diagonally across the hot sand toward the base of the piers, and steering around between the encampments. They were giggling, bumping shoulders as they laughed. Steve and I followed them through the clusters of beach gear and prostrate people, some of whom looked as if they had collapsed there under the weight of the sunshine. A woman in a bright orange bikini, a white topknot in her hair, sprayed herself with some kind of aerosol, then lay back and put on headphones, she too going limp.

The Manhattan Beach Pier looked Florentine to me, more delicate than, say, the pier at Santa Monica. We climbed up to it, up concrete steps out of the sand and past a line-up of public showers, where people in bathing suits were washing off the salt. Foot traffic crowded the paved surface of the pier, people in sunglasses and fishermen and couples and families and kids and gawking tourists. We walked toward the pier's far end, where there was an octagonal, open-air cantina with a terra-cotta roof.

Below us on the sand on the south side stood a tented pavilion where an athletic competition was going on, a running and swimming race for women. The tent fluttered with commercial banners, one reading "Speedo." Some of the contestants milled around outside, wearing yellow bathing caps and numbers on their swimsuits. They were waiting for the race to begin, some of them stretching their legs or shaking the muscles in their arms.

At the end of the pier, we bought Oranginas and sun-flower seeds as "Sledgehammer" poured from the speakers behind the counter. Then we walked back, standing at the railing to watch the race. From above, the water looked more transparent, and I could watch the swell lift yellow fingers of kelp into the light. The waves seemed to have gotten bigger. One of them broke a surfer's board down there. He was fine, for a second, dropping into a particularly big swell. Then it crunched over all at once, pounding him under and snapping his board in half with a bassy crack that made the crowd on the pier groan. When he surfaced and saw the damage, he thrashed the water with his arms, crying out.

A voice on a loudspeaker directed our attention to the starting line. A hundred or so contestants had lined up facing us several hundred yards down the beach. They would run down the beach and back, the voice told us, then swim out around the red buoys. Back on shore they would run up and down the beach again, to the finish line. A long pause proceeded, the line of women poised, then at the tiny snap of a pistol, they began, their progress at that distance mincing and furious.

Just then Steve tapped me on the shoulder and said something. I had to say "What?" and he said again, "There's your friend Lloyd." Steve pointed down the pier, but the crowd had evidently resealed itself in the time it had taken me to comprehend. Then I went blindly into the crowd, looking for Lloyd, part of me sure Steve was wrong—How would he know Lloyd? I still was thinking—and part of me already feeling delighted to see Lloyd here after conjuring him up all weekend and a little sheepish about this coincidence of running into him when I was supposed to be hundreds of miles away.

I spotted him. He was wearing white, except for his creamsicle orange baseball cap, and standing casually, slack as Fred Astaire, facing the north railing as almost everyone else faced south to watch the race. He was looking through a small, inexpensive camera, snapping a picture of the beach, recording the general scene, as if he were a visitor from Spokane.

I sidled up behind him as he concentrated on taking the picture and asked quietly, "Lloyd, are you working today?" He glanced around, giving me a look of mild annoyance until he realized who I was, then shouting "Jimmy!" and throwing his arms around me.

"You caught me in LA," I said, and Lloyd laughed, glad to have done so. "You caught me," he said. He was working, it turned out, developing a proposal for an art project at the pier. He was with a group of artists, all competing for a public commission. He gestured at the receding crowd and said, "That's my tour."

He had to go with them, he meant. And so I said goodbye, love to Louise, great seeing you, and we parted as precipitously as we'd met, Lloyd turning once, before he disappeared into the sunny crowd, to exclaim, "I never come here!" and gesturing with his arms outward to indicate the place where he certainly seemed to be in any case, there on the Manhattan Beach Pier.

Then I went back to the others, who were still watching the women's race. "What was Lloyd doing here?" asked Les. I said, "Working," and explained, still delighted. By now the swimming women were out in the blue water, their hundred yellow caps bobbing beyond the break of the waves and their arms threshing the sea in a kind of absolute anti-unison that had its own singularity, intense and full of intention.

The odds of it, I was thinking, of running into Lloyd, out of all the millions who might be on that pier that Sunday. And not only out of those millions on that day, but out of all possibilities. Our meeting on the pier could seem then like the luckiest billiard shot of all times, a last click in a chain of events that included my grandfather's coming to California and his grandfather the gambler's heading west also. Linked in that chain would be all the momentary choices, his deciding to be an artist and meeting Louise and my returning to California and making similar decisions and meeting Louise as well. Everything had to happen in exactly that way, to make this moment happen out of the infinitude of possibilities, those human odds further mul-tiplied by the purely physical chances that these particular atoms of matter would ever mingle at one tiny point in the universe. Everything had to happen like that, and it had.

Running into Lloyd let me feel that the huge forces that seemed to reduce our life on the earth to the tiniest of absurdities might actually counterbalance themselves somehow, leaving it up to us in any case. Looking down from the pier, I remembered that Pascal had written that a man was the middle point between nothing and everything, incapable of perceiving either the void from which he had emerged or the infinity in which he found himself engulfed. With my medieval mind I knew that I could not know.

Still, this weekend, capped by this coincidence of running into Lloyd, had renewed my old assurance. Uncertainty could be crushing, but in the face of infinite uncertainty, one's very existence had to seem miraculous. Beyond a certain point of unlikeliness, you had to feel safe. Having run into Lloyd anyway, I could feel amazed that bits of matter could have intentions at all. It was funny sometimes when they did, when a hundred women in yellow caps might minutely churn the azure surface of the sea.

I couldn't explain this to my friends just then, though it made me feel love for them. After all, here we were. We watched the racers swim in through the surf, some of them struggling, some riding in on the waves. I felt relaxed, there in the sunshine, really for the first time all weekend. The women began sprinting as soon as they could stand, throwing water with their knees. They ran up the slope of the beach, around a flag in the sand, then away from us, around another flag, then back to the finish line, the first runner sheer sinew down to her bare feet. We applauded and watched the lagging racers emerge for a while, all of them coming in at last just where they came in.

Les gave me a handful of sunflower seeds, and I ate them

one at a time. I liked sunflower seeds, but they were a lot of blind work and almost bitter with salt at first. I cracked one sideways in my teeth, then separated the shell from the meat with my tongue, not sure of my success until the last, when I was able to swallow the seed and spit out the light, striped husk, which twirled in the breeze as it fell down toward the water out of sight.

The Will of the Wisp

Life begins in chaos, each of us falling out of random chance, then getting the feeling that certainly we had to happen. So ever after, the way is our saying so, as seemingly firm and airborne as the Golden Gate. Hume's Way—also Ockham's and Cage's—this was the Path of the Suckhole, the surrender to the beyond, the discipline of irresolution and momentary amazement. And a crowded avenue it was, too, like the road to Canterbury, from one thing along to the next.

Hume would have liked hearing that systems on their way to chaos converge at constant rates, even if only mathematically. It would have amused him, too, to learn that any given section of coastline proves infinitely long. Should you take a micrometer to limn the shore, measuring every grain and every hollow in every pebble, the coast would prove the longer the finer the tool. No matter what, you'd find, you had to set the scale first.

You had to start somewhere, though to go on after that, to relinquish enough space for everything—yourself included—to live, you had to acknowledge first principles as essentially arbitrary, and to see that others had necessarily taken such arbitrary positions to make their own beginnings. It was as if we felt the firm step, but then stood in midair. It had to be and it had to be dismissed, just as there had to be a moment in a healthy life when the self appeared among others, relative to the overall scheme. This was the recognition. But it wasn't going to come naturally—at least to medieval me.

Me, I'd been putting the stuff I couldn't understand over there, which had seemed to allow me to work undistracted, over here, on what might be intelligible. Locke had cut that deal for science, saying nothing exists in the mind not first presented to the senses, and delivering us thereby into a universe if anything more mysterious than ever, in which we might imagine yet farther edges, yet smaller particles and—behold!—find them, as the unintelligible continued to loom beyond, the depth, the dark matter, the not, God even, whatever we decided initially wasn't in the picture. Who sees the ratio sees himself only, Blake had said. Also, that only the infinite can satisfy.

$\mathcal{L}$ikewise, in the context of my thinking over that weekend in LA, the feeling that arose from the coincidence of running into Lloyd on the pier seemed enlarged. Such a feeling had actually filled my life, I thought, *was* the feeling of being alive. An astonishing association of moments— each a complete explanation—might reveal itself in any point in time. Life could be a constant amazement, if you could let it. I, anyway, hadn't. I'd taken a position, copped some historical attitude. This was my essential yet arbitrary first step, my medieval outlook. Afterward, it occurred to me that I might be able to hold onto this insight if I attempted an account of it. Usually one didn't. Really basic assumptions seemed so evanescent, for one thing, always appearing from one's own angle only, as it were and, no matter what, fleeting as well, gone right away, even as one thought to speak. But despite such subjectivity and brevity—brevity was the kicker—the assumption behind a given ordinary moment was always particular and elaborate as well, connected as it was to many other moments. Accounting for such might require something like a novel.

There'd be gaps, as I'd just have to gesture to some of it, though all of it would contribute to this sensation I'd arrived at, there on the pier, that having a medieval mind wasn't so bad, so long as you knew you had one. It meant that there were no absolutes even in a universe of absolute chaos. You could take comfort in coincidence. You could find certainty anyway. You had to. You would.

So I could lean into chaos, fall into the sea of chance with faith in my medieval swimming ability, my gift of finding my fate wherever I went. I could stop speculating and let the moment have its meaning—or not, as the case might be. I could give in, could live, could get a life, as they say in LA. I would be medieval, an anchorite among my icons. As far as I knew, chaos was God's most delicate creation.

The Shower

At the foot of the pier, a half-dozen people were showering in public, a startling sight, even though they were wearing their swimsuits. They washed their bodies as they would in private, each with an inward gaze and with motions practiced alone, and each an emblem just then of solitary, idiosyncratic routine, the ways one found to proceed in a body on the earth, subject to gravity, revolving in space. Later, after I swam, I took a shower there myself.

Back at our encampment on the sand, I'd taken off my shoes and walked down to the water. At first I'd just wanted to stand in the ocean, to be just slightly offshore. I waded out to ankle depth, standing on the cold, pebbly bottom, my feet washed by the waves. This was as far as you could go and still be in the United States, I remembered from my childhood somewhere. Then one wave engulfed me, its frigid current imparting another fleeting sense, also from childhood, of these waves having broken every second forever and me having just arrived.

After that I had to go all the way in. Some people edge into the sea, assuming the chill a half-step at a time and hopping the waves, but I could never take that slow torture. So I plunged, yelping and diving, then swimming out past my depth. I had to swim beneath two waves before I could surface safely beyond the break. There I treaded water and lay on my back, waiting for the big ones that would break out this far, and when a set did arrive, trying to bodysurf and mostly getting worked, as the surfers say.

I had to remember again how to stroke into the wave at the right moment, so that I could fall out of its face just as it went critical. I had to stroke at the right moment, and from the right place, which varied a little from wave to wave. Too far in and the wave would crush me; too far out and it would pass unbroken beneath. Eventually I got it right once or twice, and got just an instantaneous glance up at the wave's curling hook, before it broke on me and threw me forward, bouncing and blind in the turbulence.

Then afterwards I'd wanted to wash the salt off and I walked back across the sand to those showers, carrying dry clothes in a bag. The cold blast shocked me at first and then felt intensely pleasurable, my skin smooth and flexible again as the sticky crust dissolved and cool where the sun had singed it. In the dressing room I pushed my hair back with a brush and stripped off the purple shorts, which, drenched, were slick as a skin themselves.

I pulled out those white pants. They'd improved on the trip, I thought. Brightened and softened, furred a little by the bleach, they came crumpled from the bag.

J-Outer

Across from me in the gate sat a woman wearing three wooden dolls strung with beads around her neck. Each doll bore a name: Kara, Janis, Alison, the letters vertical. In the corridor an airport attendant pushed an empty wheelchair. A couple came in, she pregnant and he with a toddler in a backpack. Bugs Bunny looked out of the Warner Brothers logo on the front of a guy's black T-shirt. Those swoopy Z-shaped eyeglass frames, one woman had on. The airport attendant returned, pushing the same wheelchair, in it now a man wearing a plaid shirt, mostly orange. The woman in the Z-shaped frames had a pin on her lapel in the shape of a rooster. In the line that formed at the ticket counter a woman in black nudged her bag forward with the side of her foot. In the corridor, two Muslim women swathed in kerchiefs went by. A really tall man in a blue suit, his garment bag on his shoulder, puffed through his lower lip, poofing his bangs. Les went to buy a magazine and came back with *Vogue*. Hundreds and hundreds of strangers went about their business in the airport, each one radiating the entire universe. The plane was jammed, every seat filled. A man spoke Japanese to his seated wife as he pressed his bag into the overhead bin, while a woman in black cowboy boots with silver tips waited behind him in the aisle, and on the PA Mr. Gerald Wellham was asked to raise his hand. All of us, each of us, about to fly.

We'd gotten off the beach as the day had drawn down, the four of us hauling the gear back to the cars, a longer walk than it had seemed on the way there. Jess and Steve had planned to stop at Bristol Farms before they went home, and having a little time, we had followed them in the Pontiac to the store. Again we passed through the LA landscape, block after block of minimarts and mom-and-pop stores, boutiques and restaurants and manicure shops. By then I could see each of these places as the economic center of someone's life.

How could they all stay in business? I wondered. Where in the world was the volume? Could there possibly be, back there where they actually lived, in the houses behind the avenue facades of dry cleaners and Christian bookstores, enough odd need, enough people coming forth from their homes each day on some pilgrimage that held the world together for a second—to rent a video game, to restock on Bounty—enough customers, anyway, to keep all these little shops in business? Evidently so. It seemed a miracle just then, like the loaves and fishes, though it was so everyday as to be invisible once you got used to it. In its ordinary way it was magnificent, like a terrific levitation act in which what gets levitated is a blue Dodge minivan.

We had dispersed in the fancy supermarket, looking at things. I'd sampled sausages and slices of mango, got a ticket at the bakery counter and asked for Jewish rye bread—real New York bread, which is hard to find in San Francisco. I'd glimpsed the others in the aisles as I'd wandered, though when Les found me to say that it was time to go to the airport, we hadn't been able to find Steve in the big store at first, and couldn't leave until we did of course, and then had to have a quick good-bye, thanking them and hugging them in the supermarket parking lot.

On the plane, we'd sat just behind the wing, which had looked delicate enough out there, its stabilizers pointing backward and its flaps bladelike, edges thin as wafers to enhance the pilot's control to that degree. The plane lurched as it began to taxi. Outside, pieces of unidentifiable technology and the numbers and lines of the airport system drifted past, as piano music tinkled beneath the sound of the whining jets. A guy in a red hat rode a bicycle on the tarmac among the huge wheels of the planes and around the clown-trains of the baggage carts. Then the hieroglyphic runway opened—the signs reading J-Outer, 3, 2—and the big jet accelerated a little, jogging over the seams in the pavement. The hills to the north looked milky, and a toddler sitting behind us somewhere said no, no, no, no, no.

When we reached the take-off point, the plane paused on the stripes—I could see sand dunes down there at the end—and my friend took my hand with her clammy one. Then the engines raced and the jet plunged ahead for a long count as Les clutched me. The big tires seemed to pluck as they lost contact with the ground. Outside, that theme restaurant and the real LAX control tower and a new one still encased in its scaffolding flew by, and then palm trees below us and the beach, the enormous ocean beyond making the land seem trivial. My ears cleared. I got a glimpse straight down of fire pits spaced at even intervals across the sand, then of waves on the shore—the same surf I'd just been in—then the open sea, its complex and delicate ripples becoming, as we gained altitude, the finest insinuation of texture on the mottled blue void, and only a ship far out steaming purposefully along to show the earth inhabited by creatures with plans.

We flew west for a long time, as if we were off to the Far East. Out ahead the sun did not seem to be sinking. Let it set, I thought, and congratulated Les, whose sheer will had delivered us through another takeoff, lifting the enormous machine into the sky. She was still concentrating and couldn't respond, so I got out my book to resume my reading at the next chapter, entitled "The Transformation of the

Modern Era." The pages there were clean and dry. The plane finally banked north, heading for home. The cart was coming down the aisle. I ordered tomato juice.

Then in less than two hours, we were back in cool San Francisco, another world from LA, though I still had beach sand in my shoes. We made dinner at home and ate some of the rye bread and afterward called Jess and Steve, who seemed very nearby then, and also phoned Louise and Lloyd. Louise said that Lloyd had made her guess and guess who it had been on the Manhattan Beach Pier. He said she'd never guess in a million years.

Acknowledgments

This idea became a book with help and encouragement from my agent, Chuck Verrill, from Jack Shoemaker, my editor and counselor at Counterpoint, and from the publisher, Frank Pearl. Others who made key contributions here are the Los Angeles residents who let me tell their stories. Thanks also to my readers, Harry Clewans, Dayna Goldfine, Dan Geller, João Almino, Holly Blake, Fritzie Brown, Frances Bowles, Carole McCurdy, and Leslie Jonath, and to Trish Hoard, Megan Butler, and Elizabeth Shreve for their work. Rabbi Chaim Fasman at Temple Kollel advised me on the meaning of sneakers and Yom Kippur. The Headlands Center for the Arts continues to be a mainstay. Richard Tarnas's fine book, *The Passion of the Western Mind*, was an inspiration for this project, and I've treated it shabbily enough, inundating it with tomato juice.

About the Author

Jim Paul is a writer and poet living in San Francisco. He is the author of two previous books, *Catapult* and *What's Called Love*. His book-length translation of a tenth-century work entitled *The Rune Poem* will appear in the spring of 1996. Jim Paul was a Guggenheim Fellow in 1994.